BLACKBERRIES
AND
CREAM

BLACKBERRIES AND CREAM

Leslie Rivver

GREEN WRITERS PRESS

Brattleboro, Vermont

Printed in the United States

10 9 8 7 6 5 4 3 2 1

Green Writers Press is a Vermont-based publisher whose
mission is to spread a message of hope and renewal through
the words and images we publish. Throughout we will adhere
to our commitment to preserving and protecting the natural
resources of the earth. To that end, a percentage of our
proceeds will be donated to environmental activist groups.
Green Writers Press gratefully acknowledges support from
individual donors, friends, and readers to help support the
environment and our publishing initiative.

Giving Voice to Writers & Artists Who Will Make the World a Better Place
Green Writers Press | Brattleboro, Vermont
www.greenwriterspress.com

ISBN: 978-09961357-7-1

Visit the author's website for more information:
www.leslierivver.com

COVER AND INTERIOR ARTWORK: Andrew Doss

PRINTED ON PAPER WITH PULP THAT COMES FROM FSC-CERTIFIED FORESTS, MANAGED FORESTS THAT
GUARANTEE RESPONSIBLE ENVIRONMENTAL, SOCIAL, AND ECONOMIC PRACTICES BY LIGHTNING SOURCE
ALL WOOD PRODUCT COMPONENTS USED IN BLACK & WHITE, STANDARD COLOR, OR SELECT COLOR
PAPERBACK BOOKS, UTILIZING EITHER CREAM OR WHITE BOOKBLOCK PAPER, THAT ARE
MANUFACTURED IN THE LA VERGNE, TENNESSEE PRODUCTION CENTER ARE
SUSTAINABLE FORESTRY INITIATIVE® (SFI®) CERTIFIED SOURCING

For Ida Bell,

who taught me

that I didn't need the coffee after all

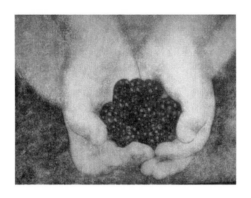

PRELUDE

This story begins and ends with grace.

I am Grace Callaway.
Just Grace, no middle name.
Daddy says that's because when I was born,
I was one hundred percent pure grace.
Nothing more, nothing less.

BLACKBERRIES
AND
CREAM

1

WHEN your own momma don't like you, it's a sad thing. No, sad isn't quite right; it's a scary thing. Today, June 11, 1965, would be the beginning of something good with my momma, I just knew it.

"Ida Bell?" my voice swelled into the upstairs hallway of our Antebellum home and I waited to hear back.

"Whoo-ooooo, up here, Gracie-girl!"

"I'm fixing to run out to the back yard for a little bit. Will's out there, and Momma's home on lunch break in the kitchen. I want to say hey to her on my way outside." Life-sized hand painted oil portraits of Will, Meri, Lisbeth, and me lined the stairwell wall.

"All right, then. I'll come on down in a minute. We gone enjoy us a picnic directly, so stay where you can hear me, child." The three-tiered fountain in the front flower garden reflected sunshine into the house, brightening the already dazzling white stairway. Perfect picnic weather.

"Yes, ma'am. I will." In three cartwheels I landed in the kitchen.

"Grace Callaway, how many times have I asked you to walk inside this house? We do not live in a circus tent," Momma said through her BLT.

I lowered my arms, opting out of the final cartwheel to the screen door. Momma had a lot of stress on her at work, and I frazzled her last nerve most of the time. "I'm sorry, Momma. Hey, Ida Bell and me are having a picnic under the big oak. Want to carry your sandwich outside and sit with us before you drive back to work? It's pretty as a twirling skirt out there." I hoped Momma'd come on out with me. She tended to pay close attention to me in front of Ida Bell.

"No, thanks, Peamite. I better not. If I go out in that soupy air, I'll drip all the way back to work." Momma and Daddy both had to look nice for work. Momma called it "being presentable." Momma worked at the Monroe County Welfare Department, and Daddy, known as "Dr. Callaway," was a college professor. For extra income, he also worked as a part-time preacher at a tiny country church on account Momma says we never have enough money. Funny thing is, we had ten times more money than anybody else I knew.

I reckon I should've known Momma's answer about coming outside before I asked the question. Studying the detail of the tile on our kitchen floor for a second, I noticed for the first time hints of blue in the stone mosaic. The floor was mostly brown on account Momma said darker colors hide dirt real well, but I spotted a blue speckled pebble and decided to point it out to Ida Bell later on. Don't know why we didn't have more of that color; there wasn't one speck of dirt needed hiding on any Callaway floor. I kissed Momma's cheek and took in her scent of Chanel N°5, rubbing my wrist on hers so I could smell her perfume all afternoon.

I dug some dog biscuits out of the five-pound bag we kept under the sink and went on out back. The door creaked shut behind me, and I steadied myself for the combination of burning-up hot air in the face and the knockdown greetings from our fourteen dogs. We couldn't turn away four of them, strays who showed up hungry and trembling. The fifth dog, Ruby-Dee, sported full-blooded German shepherd lines. She birthed nine puppies, and somehow us kids talked Momma and Daddy into letting us keep every last one of them, long as they stayed outside at all times. Which they did, except for those few times they didn't. When Momma and Daddy worked at their offices, we sometimes "accidentally" let the dogs in because it was hilarious watching every one of them race through the house in blurry streaks.

"Patches! Pug! Razz! Hi, there, sweetie pies! Go get 'em!" Throwing treats out in the yard distracted the dogs from turning me right into a mess of slobber and red-dirt paw prints. I snuck a peek inside the window to see if Momma'd seen my dog treat idea, but her eyes were glued to the twelve o'clock news on the TV set.

"Look here, Grace!" Will called, waving me over to the swing set. "Climb the ladder, hurry up!" He had put a ladder on one side of the swing set, and was walking across the top pole to reach the tree house on the other side. Crazy as it sounds, he did this all the time just like it was a big, flat sidewalk.

Ginger and Ruby-Dee wagged into a furry frenzy while I climbed the ladder out of their reach. The top of the swing set gave me a good enough place to wait for the dogs to calm down. When Will jumped out of the tree house, though, and headed for the ladder, I rolled my eyes, amazed at two things: how he hoodwinked me for the umpteenth time, and my own darn stupidity. Will was so mean, he could make a nun cuss. Now, why in the world did I go and listen to him?

"What you gone do now, Little Miss Priss?" He threw the ladder down in the grass, leaving me high and dry-mouthed, then hightailed it back up the knotted rope into the tree house to oversee my embarrassment. "Guess it's time you learned how to walk the pole like your talented big brother."

Will's contented face glowed, but I refused to look at him and give him the pleasure of thinking he'd bothered me the least little bit. Looking past him, and hoping they'd lend me a little bit of their grounding, I focused in on the steadiness of the old pines standing tall throughout the couple of acres between our house and our neighbor Mr. Whetstone's. Truth was, my insides turned to water. This was one of those problems that pure action would solve quicker than if I thought it out to death. I'd watched Will walk that blasted pole back and forth a thousand times, and even backward a time or two. If he could do it, you bet your very last nickel I could, too. I could make it to the tree house in just four or five steps.

"Grace Callaway, I could get across that pole if it was made outta hot coals. You just got to fix your eyes on this end and get on with it," he said.

"Shut up! Can't you see I'm concentrating?"

"I'm gone tell Momma you said 'shut up.' You know she don't allow that kind of talk."

"Momma's gone shut you up when she finds out you put me up here."

"Yeah, well, she won't be finding out, now will she? And if she does, you'll find your blankie-poo in the mud hole out in them woods."

Heat puddled up in my face. He had me two ways. Number one, he poked fun at me because I still slept with my baby blanket. Its faded yellows and blues stroked my face soft as blooming cotton. Number two, throwing it in the mud would thrill him to no end, hateful as he was.

The only thing harder than walking a swing set pole was keeping my balance up there with soggy feet. Mine sweated up a storm what with it being June and all. My hands left wet prints on the pole, too, on account of the fear spreading through me like a poison ivy breakout. I got to my feet, stared down the end of the pole and eased my left foot in front of my right, pretending Will wasn't standing there with his hands on his sorry hips like he was God Almighty waiting for the sinful to run down the aisle. Then my right foot edged on out front. Just three or four more steps now.

"Oh, my Lord! Grace Callaway, you get down from there right this instant, and I mean *this* instant!" Momma yelled an octave higher than usual from the screen door, waving her kitchen cloth.

I caught that bright white cloth out the corner of my eye and lost track of the end of the pole. Before I could say, "But Momma," I tumbled down and landed smack-dab on my back. Pain whopped me between my shoulder blades and spread throughout the rest of me like a windshield shattering from a stray rock. My breath whooshed up into the sky. For the life of me, I couldn't pull it back in. The blue up above swirled around like a kaleidoscope picture, a sure sign I was headed to Glory to gather my rewards. Will yelled out something I can't repeat, then crouched down in the tree house, out of sight and he hoped, out of Momma's mind. Once my breath found me again, smelling fresh-cut grass gave me a little comfort. I figured Glory, and the road getting there, wouldn't smell like yard work. I closed my eyes and tears squeezed out.

2

IDA BELL'S face appeared like a fairy godmother, smoothing out the broken blue above me. She squinted her eyes and got that wrinkle on her forehead she only gets when she's real serious about something. She studied my face and then the rest of me, then scooped me up and carried me over to the porch swing. I tried to give her a little smile; I'd rather roll around on nails than see that wrinkle on Ida Bell's forehead. When she realized I was all right, she drew in a deep breath and yelled up to Will, "Get your sad self out of that there tree house and on down to your room, Will Callaway. Don't you be letting me see your front or your back end until after band practice, you hear?"

"Yes, ma'am," he said, his gaze not meeting mine or Ida Bell's. I let my eyes and my world rest for just a minute there in Ida Bell's hold. The hot sun and all it kept alive sent a soothing stroke over my aching body. Then a scent so familiar, a scent that entranced me and then ran off like a fox in the wild, gave my eyes a reason to open back up. Chanel N°5.

"Ida Bell, what in God's name was she doing up on the very top of that swing set? Is she all right?" Momma asked, and the hint of a sunny yellow thrill waved from my top to my toes. Momma had ventured out in that drippy air to see about *me*.

"Well, now, she a little banged up, but we gone see to it," Ida Bell said. "And let me tell you, we ain't gone be seeing Mr. Will no time soon. That boy'll keep outta my sight if he knows what's good for him."

"All right, then. I'm gone."

I wanted my mother to stay right here, like sometimes the way I needed a song to keep on playing, scared of the silence when it ends. But Momma stayed tangled up these days, and the quiet between us was beginning to get right loud. I didn't even care if I only got time with her because I was hurt, long as she sat by me for just a minute or two.

I puffed my cheeks with air and held my breath, determined not to get to crying all over again. Momma's words squeezed hard at my heart. *I'm gone. I'm gone. I'm gone.* She sure enough was gone, right out to work and right away from my arms that ached more to hold on to her than they did from any stupid fall on account of my sorry ol' brother.

"Gracie-girl, you hurt anywhere, little darling?" Ida Bell said.

"All over. Bass drums are beating in my head and the rest of me feels broke apart."

"All right, now. Let's me and you sit a spell." She sang "Precious Lord" to the rhythm of the swaying swing. Her gentle hands running through my hair calmed me like the voiceless words of pine trees in the wind.

Glancing past Ida Bell's arms, I kept an eye on Momma while she freshened up her lipstick and headed for the car. She had time to make herself look pretty? That was more important than seeing about me? It occurred to me that my sisters never got time with Momma, either, but it didn't seem to gnaw at them like it did me.

Ida Bell broke into my thoughts, "Gracie-girl, you and me gone even the score with that rascal brother of yours." She helped me over to the picnic quilt under the big shady oak, then disappeared inside.

I got real cozy watching the wind sway the silvery moss on the old tree. Its branches grew so thick they could be trees all by themselves. From the main trunk, the branches arched above me and reached over to the ground, creating my very own tree fort. It wrapped the warm Alabama air around me like loving arms, and if that just didn't beat all. Here I was getting all hugged on by a tree, but not by my own momma.

I sniffed my wrist for Chanel N°5, then caught myself up in a daydream about Momma picking me up after I fell off that swing set and letting me rest my head on her shoulder, not worrying one bit about tears or snot or red Alabama dirt getting on her bleach-white linen blouse. When I came to, I wondered what would happen if I curled up and played dead like the resurrection fern growing on the oak. All it needed was just a little hint of water, and it would spring right straight back to life.

Ida Bell showed back up with banana sandwiches, sliced tomatoes, and coffee. Coffee-drinking was our little secret, and every time we shared it, I stirred cream in until my coffee blended in with Ida Bell's skin color, hoping it would turn my skin sugary-brown just like hers. Ida Bell was also carrying the cookies Will always hid in a basket on top of the fridge, a big green tin that said "Pure Lard" on the front, and a mischievous look in her eye.

"Ida Bell, what's 'Pure Lard'?"

She grinned wide as her stained-glass-blue Cadillac. "This here gone serve as your brother's new cookie stuffing, Gracie-girl. Now, don't that favor cookie stuffing to you?" she asked, opening the tin so I could peek inside.

"Looks exactly like cookie stuffing to me. I mean *exactly*." My aching body sure enough began to bounce. I sniffed for Momma's scent again, but caught wind of Ida Bell's rosy-smelling perfume instead. My heart didn't ache quite so bad for Momma, what with Ida Bell right here and all.

Will lived for Oreo cookies, maybe even more than he lived for his marching band. This week, Daddy shopped for groceries in place of Momma on account of one of her sinking spells from a hard day's work. Daddy bought a super-saver bag of Big 60 cookies instead of Momma's usual Oreos. "Now, Will's done turned red in the face about not having them Oreo cookies, but he still standing over them cheap ones like they's the last thing to eat on God's green earth," Ida Bell said.

"Yeah, if he sees me going near them, he says he's gone eat

every last one and then turn around and tell Momma and Daddy it was me."

"Well, he gone learn himself a little lesson this time."

Between sips of creamy coffee and bites of lunch, Ida Bell and me scraped every drop of stuffing out of those cookies and spread Pure Lard inside them instead. Then we put them back so they looked the same as always.

"He gone wish he hadn't acted so selfish with them cookies, now, ain't he, Gracie-girl, and Mr. Big Britches sure enough gone wish he hadn't put you up on that swing set!" Ida Bell said with a slap on her knee.

"Yes, ma'am!" I said, and we shook hands in our secret way. I made a sign language <u>G</u> for my name. Ida Bell made an <u>I</u> for hers. We linked our fingers and shook like a handshake.

❧ 3 ❧

TOWARDS late afternoon, Ida Bell and me piddled around in the kitchen so we'd be close by when Will came home from marching band practice. Using fresh blackberries Ida Bell and her grandkids picked that very morning, we worked on three cobblers right from scratch: one for us Callaways, one for Ida Bell to carry home, and the third for her to share at the Pecan Grove Baptist Church's Wednesday evening potluck.

Will bounced into the kitchen with a hot, red face and his band buddy, Ben. He always looked half-dead after practice; sometimes I secretly wished for his other half to go on and die, too. As sure as the day was long, he reached right up to the top of the fridge for "his" cookies, and then inside the fridge for icy-cold dipping milk. He and Ben both flopped down at the table with long, drawn out breaths.

Ida Bell filled up the pie dishes with the berry mixture while I cut half-inch strips of rolled-out dough for the lattice crust. I didn't look at her, and she didn't look at me. It was hard enough not to act like something was going on, but one look at each other, and we'd double over laughing and give away our secret.

"Now, Ben, this here's the best treat east of the Mississippi," Will said, dipping a cookie and handing it to his friend. His face was happy as a tick on a fat dog. He dunked one for himself, too, and popped it whole right into his mouth. Ida Bell and me kept our heads down and our hands hard at work, laying down seven parallel dough strips across each pie.

It only took half a chew before Will and Ben both tasted the Pure Lard. Ben spit his into his napkin and guzzled some milk, but Will—well he carried on like somebody chased after him with a BB gun. He flinched and flailed this way and that, and turned even redder in the face than before, a fire lit behind his eyes. He flew off the handle, "Ida Bell, somebody went and put lard in my cookies, and they just better watch out!" I studied the crisscross pattern on my pie, pretending it needed fixing. I wanted to look up at Will something terrible, but I knew better. If I did, the giggles that were squished down in my belly would sure enough jump on out.

"Now, why somebody gone go and do a fool thing like that?" Ida Bell asked, an earnest look in her eye and not even cracking one hint of a smile.

He kicked at the floor and set his hands on both hips. "I couldn't tell you, but I won't get that awful taste out of my mouth for a solid week."

Ida Bell crossed her fingers behind her back. "Child, ain't nobody done put lard in them cookies," she said. "You starting to sound like you done gone 'round the bend a little bit. Must have made a mistake at the factory. Now, why don't you go visit the good folks down at the Piggly Wiggly and see won't they give you a fresh bag."

"All right, then. I will. Let's go, Ben." They left with their Pure Lard cookies, spitting in the yard every other step.

When the boys were just far enough away, Ida Bell and me cut loose. Our giggles had us in pain and reaching for tissues to blot our eyes. And just when one of us would pull back together, the other would start laughing all over again, the way laughing can't be stopped for nothing during a church service. "It worked, Ida Bell!" I finally managed to say, with a satisfaction that darn near only comes from beating the boys in the running races on field day.

"Course it did, Gracie-girl," she said, that we-know-what-we're-doing sort of smile across her face. "Course it did."

Giggling in between, we finished up weaving the lattice crust, crimped the edges, and then sprinkled a little cane sugar on top. "Now, Gracie, you go on and put a little more sugar than it calls for. Way I figure, if a little bit tastes good, a little bit more gone be even better!" Ida Bell said, a twinkle like stardust in her eyes.

While the cobblers baked and filled up the air with pie-crust scent like holiday time, we took turns reading to each other from the funny papers in *The Monroe Journal*. We read until Momma and Daddy came home from work. Once Momma disappeared into the bedroom to change out of her work clothes, Daddy asked a question right off. "Ida Bell, Will called my office all riled up, something about lard in his cookies. Do you know what he was talking about?"

"Well, sure I do, Dr. Callaway. He had lard in his cookies, sure as I'm standing here. I sent him down to the Piggly Wiggly to get it straightened out."

"That's why he called me. Said the good folks at the Piggly Wiggly didn't take too kindly to being accused of larding-up his cookies. They told him and Ben that their behavior was bordering on harassment, and said if they came around again with make-believe trouble, they'd call the law on them."

The light in Ida Bell's eyes grew a shade brighter, but only I would notice such a thing. "Mmm-mmm, that boy sure do know how to stir up some trouble. You hear about him putting Gracie here up to walking the top pole of the swing set?"

"I did," Daddy said, scrunching up his mouth and reaching out for me. "You back to feeling all right, Gracie?"

I hugged Daddy tight and winked at Ida Bell behind his back. "I sure am, Daddy. I'm feeling mighty good." Daddy couldn't see Ida Bell and me smiling at each other. She and I both made our letters for our handshake, and did an imaginary shake from a distance so Daddy wouldn't know we'd been up to something.

I drifted to sleep that night some kind of satisfied. Ida Bell had helped me get back at Will a bunch of times, but something about it happening in front of one of his friends put a cherry on top of my sundae.

❧   ❧

It seemed like I'd only slept a few minutes when the dogs woke me, barking up a blue streak and howling like the moon had dropped right out of the night sky. I thought I was dreaming, but as I came to, I realized that flickers of light shone through Lisbeth's and my bedroom window where there ought to have been dark. It slowly dawned on me that something was wrong.

I checked the clock: 2:58 A.M. Grabbing the picture of Ida Bell I kept under my pillow, I waved aside my pink curtains and the sparkly yellow star that hung in the window for wishing on. Then, I froze. Wheaton Whetstone's house was nothing but a heap of tall orange flames lapping up toward the stars. His place stood about the length of a football field from ours, but the pines in between gave fire to each other like hands passing an offering plate. Their popping, cracking, and sizzling sent a shiver straight through my middle. The hair on my arms stood up. I held my picture of Ida Bell close and ran for help.

"Lisbeth! Momma! Daddy! Momma!" My screams got stuck in my throat. I shouted, all right, but they came out like measly little whispers. I tossed Lisbeth's covers off her, gave her a shake, then ran to Momma and Daddy's room and grabbed Momma's arm. She sat straight up in bed, wild in her eyes and her mouth all scrunched up.

"Land sakes, what's going on, Grace?" Momma said, her arms holding both my shoulders like she needed to shake some sense into me. I pulled her into mine and Lisbeth's room and before I even pointed outside, Momma found her scream. "William, get the kids! Get them out of here! Whet's house is burning up and ours is next!"

"Oh, my word!" Daddy yelled.

"I've got Grace. Meet me out front with the big kids. Hurry, William. *Hurry!*"

❧ 4 ❧

I'D NEVER in my entire life seen fear across my Daddy's face, and that right there made me even more scared than I already was. The color drained out of his cheeks, and his eyes, usually all full of pooly blue, showed their whites. "Lisbeth, run get Meri and wait on me at the front door. I'll be there with Will in just a minute," he said, not blinking.

Will had converted the basement into his bedroom a few years back on account he needed his privacy. It was a hike from way up here, two flights of stairs and several stretches of hallway in between. I took back the thought I had earlier about the other half of Will dying. I wasn't so sure, though, that a person could really and truly take back a thought. Once it's been thought, it just might always be out there no matter what. Daddy turned into a blurry streak, running down the hallway and out of sight.

"Momma, should I get some things? The photo albums?" I asked.

"The only thing you need to *get* is yourself out the front door, Grace Callaway." Momma held my arm so tight it hurt. All I could think about was the painting Ida Bell gave me for my fifth birthday. It was a watercolor of me and her out in the blackberry patch, the sunshine lighting up the berries and our faces. She painted it her very own self. When I unwrapped it, she let out a little giggle. Said her husband told her it looked liked a child had painted it. "And I done told him I sure do love children's paintings, and he couldn't have paid me a better compliment!" she said. Didn't nothing get Ida Bell's feathers ruffled. I wanted so bad to go get that painting. Plus, getting out of the house before Daddy made it out with everybody else was the same as leaving them behind and I didn't like it one bit.

Momma pulled me down the stairs and out the front door. We sprinted toward the road, the wind sending smoke up our noses, and our driveway stretching out longer than it ever had before. I counted the oak trees as we made our way. We have twenty, ten on each side, every last one of them bowing in submission to the wind and choking smoke. The air was clearer out on Daisy Street where we stopped to catch our breath and watch the house for Daddy and the rest. Light from the fire made shadows of the big oaks reach at our house like long, crimpy monster arms. I looked down at my picture of Ida Bell and whispered, "I love you." I wondered if it was me telling her, or her telling me.

Somebody ran down Daisy Street toward our house, but the dark kept me from seeing who. "Sadie, y'all all right?" I recognized Bev's voice, Momma's good friend from up the road. Bev's oldest daughter, Harper, had been my best friend on Daisy Street since we were thumb-sucking babies. They lived just on the other side of Wheaton Whetstone.

"We're fine, Bev. Y'all okay?" Momma said.

"Everybody's out of the house, but look at those flames, and Sadie, look at which way the wind is moving!" Momma and me both eyed the treetops between the fire and our house. Every last pine and oak swayed toward the house like waves headed to the shore. With the wind behaving all wild, Wheaton Whetstone's house acted like a blowtorch exhaling fire right into our woods. All my nerves rattled and bunched up in my feet. I jumped in place, wishing to high heavens Daddy'd show himself on up.

"Sadie, I'm gone run back up to the house and gather up everybody on Daisy Street I can find. We'll hurry back to save what we can from your place," Bev said. "And Sadie? Nobody's seen hide nor hair of Whet." Bev shook her head and wiped sweat from rolling into her eyes. Then she disappeared back into the night.

I stared into them flames jumping out the windows of Wheaton Whetstone's place. Biggest fire I've ever seen in all my ten years; maybe the biggest fire ever to burn in all the world. Even the second story was nothing but bright orange, alive and hungry and mean. The attic billowed haunted smoke, and its skeleton hung there like a secret never told to nobody. I expected to see Mr. Whetstone jump from one of them windows, or drive down the road in his car after having gone to fetch the fire fighters. It was beyond me to think of him inside there all by himself.

"Sadie? Grace?" Daddy's voice rambled through the trees.

"Over here by the road, William!" Momma called out.

My eyes burned from the gathering smoke. When I finally caught sight of Daddy with Lisbeth, Meri, and Will, my shoulders lowered and I drew in a deep breath hoping to get my heart out of my throat. In the distance, Route 21 was all lit up parade-like with big red engines speeding toward Daisy Street and sirens acting rude to the quiet of nighttime. I closed my burning eyes, and for a minute pretended we were at a Fourth of July party instead of watching Mr. Whetstone's house burn to the ground, and waiting for ours to go next.

Then I remembered. The back yard was fenced in. A trembling, crazed sensation swept from the top of my head to the bottom of my feet. I kissed my picture of Ida Bell and put it in my pocket, then shook loose from Momma's hold and took off toward the house again. "The dogs!" I yelled. Looking at them flames, I thought the world might end, but there was no way it was gonna end for my dogs. Not like this.

5

"GRACE CALLAWAY, get back here, and I mean *this instant!*" Momma yelled, but I kept straight on running like my feet had sprouted wings. I fixed my eyes on the left side of the house, the side away from the fire. If I kept sight of the torchlight that always stayed on by the garage, I could get there, smoke or not.

With prayers for thoughts, I ran down the driveway until I passed the creek that runs through everybody's front yard on our side of Daisy Street. My hands flashed one at a time in front of my face from my arms pumping so hard. I cut across the oaks on the left. The torchlight came and went through the stinging haze, but I held its picture in my memory and found the garage. The stitch in my side doubled me over until Ruby-Dee's familiar bark got me moving again.

"I'm coming, girl! Come on to the gate, now!" She gave a discerning yelp, and I knew she understood. That dog was right smart. I loved those strays and Ruby-Dee's puppies, but right now all I counted on was Ruby-Dee. If she met me at the gate, all thirteen of the others would follow her like she was everybody's momma.

I ducked my head inside my shirt, trying to find some air that didn't clog up my chest. My lungs were suffocating like I was stuck under a pillow, so I dropped to the ground to catch some cleaner air, then held my breath until I found the gate. The latch lifted right up, and Ruby-Dee knocked me down while the others gathered 'round. I couldn't see anymore, couldn't breathe anymore.

Just then, sturdy and determined arms lifted me off the ground and into the truck. Daddy! He gave one whistle, and every last dog jumped into the truck bed like they'd practiced the drill a hundred times. I sucked in the clean air inside the truck like pink lemonade. Cuts I didn't even know I got while I ran down the gravel driveway burned streaks on the bottoms of my feet. My coughs wouldn't let up.

"Are you breathing all right, Gracie?" Daddy said.

"I'm better now that we're in here. We got all the dogs, didn't we, Daddy?"

"All fourteen, we surely did. *You* did, sweetheart."

I didn't have no more energy left for crying, or I would have just then. My Daddy was sweeter than fresh-picked sugarcane. I closed my eyes and felt the weight of his hand resting on my back. "Daddy, we'd better hurry back to Momma or she'll have all of Daisy Street looking for us." Then he quoted,

Let us go then, you and I

I picked up where he left off best as I could,

When the evening is spread out against the sky

Daddy loved beautiful words and meaningful thoughts, especially when the two came together. I was only ten years old, but I bet I knew more lines of poetry than most adults on account of him. Before I could even pronounce the words right, Daddy'd start a poem and let me finish it.

By the time we reached Momma, fire trucks lined all of Daisy Street, their red engines lit up from the blaze and spinning lights. Firefighters with glow-in-the-dark stripes on their gear aimed heavy hoses at Whet Whetstone's house. Flames spilled out of there like demons running out of hell. Four workers sprayed our burning pines, two of them aiming for the trunks and two for the branches and crowns. Others stood at attention, waiting with their hoses in front of our house, across the street at the Faulkner's, and up at Harper's place, just in case.

"Y'all stay near the stream," a firefighter yelled. "This fire's alive and on the move!" We headed closer to the water. My nerves were shot, and my legs gave way. I stumbled into Momma, and a whiff of Chanel N°5 put a little hope back into my heart.

Four more firefighters came over to our woods, carrying tools that looked like a hoe on one side and a rake on the other. Two of them raked a vertical line between our house and Mr. Whetstone's. The other two hacked at our little trees and the azalea bushes that made the piney woods look like a miracle in early spring.

"What on earth are they doing, Daddy?" I asked.

"They're making a fire line so the fire won't have any fuel to burn. They're trying their hardest to save our home."

"But what about the big ol' pines still spreading flames?" Before Daddy said a word, I got my answer. The roar of two chainsaws revving up turned my head. I'd never seen anything like it in my entire life. First one, then another. They were cutting down our pine trees! What I didn't get was how those firefighters made the trees fall in the direction of Wheaton Whetstone's house what with the wind carrying on in the other direction. They must've felled ten or so trees, each one making a rainbow of fire in the sky on its way to the ground. Every time one fell, a firefighter from the street doused it straight off with water.

Bev came on back to our place with all of Daisy Street behind her. I knew Harper was all right, but seeing her face did me some good. "Harper, hey! I can't believe all this, can you?"

"Oh my gosh, Grace! I couldn't even see your house from mine." Harper held out her arms and I reached up to give her a hug. She was the tallest person I knew. I was the shortest person she knew. Daddy always said if Harper tripped and fell at our house, she was so tall she'd land halfway home. Always dressed like it was Easter Sunday, Harper had on a pale pink nightgown with pretty flutter sleeves and a matching tiered robe with satin trim. She even had on her little princess slippers to match. I gave her a hard time. "Where's your pink hair ribbons to go with that? We might make the front page of the *Monroe Journal*, you know!"

Harper grinned, and kept hold of my shoulders. "We saw the fire chief on the way down the street," she said. "He said for y'all not to worry about trying to save things."

"Why not?"

"He said he knew it didn't look like it, but they were close to having Mr. Whetstone's fire put out." She reached out and gave me another hug, and I took in the deepest breath I could ever remember.

We all stood in a huddle near the flowing water, not particularly talking too much, but watching and wanting to stay together just the same. We tried to balance feeling thankful that no one else's house caught fire and feeling anxious about Mr. Whetstone and his place. I stuck my hand in my pocket and held tight to my picture of Ida Bell. I sure wished she was clustered there with us right then.

"Lord, have mercy," Bev said to Momma. "They still haven't got sight of Whet. Got an ambulance waiting up the road there."

"You know, Bev, Whet had more money than the Father, the Son, and the Holy Ghost put together. I guess money can't always save a person," Momma said.

"His money was new money, though. Whet never did seem to know how to act around us folks with old, bona-fide money. He was a good man, though."

"I swanee, I guess you're right. But now isn't it something that a person like Whet, using his financial standing to study preaching the Good Word, would suffer such a thing as this?"

"It most certainly is, Sadie. I just don't know." They both stared into the ashy clouds, raising their eyebrows at God.

Dawn rolled in about the time things calmed down. The streetlights blinked off one by one, and I hoped that Ida Bell would show up soon. With the brightening sky, I could see that the leftover flickers on Wheaton Whetstone's house couldn't reach ours anymore. The only thing there was the concrete foundation and charred, haunted shapes that once meant something to somebody.

Mr. Whetstone burned right up with his house. The fire chief said they found his leftover body heaped up in his library. Said he most likely died of smoke inhalation before he suffered a single burn, and that made me feel some better. The chief also said Mr. Whetstone was huddled over something he wanted to protect, a book maybe, one with a leather cover. I had never known anybody who died before now, but I couldn't imagine a person caring for something in a burning house to the point they was willing to reach heaven early on its account. I would've got my Ida Bell painting if Momma'd let me, but my house wasn't full of flames like Whet's. Those dogs, though? I reckon I'd have burned up with the house like Whet to save them. Maybe that was the bravest thing I've ever done. Bravery was a new feeling to me, and I liked that it was me being brave this time instead of admiring the bravery of Lisbeth, Meri, or Will.

❧ 6 ❧

"LISBETH, did you hear the fire chief talking about Whet Whetstone being hovered over something when they found him?" I asked, sticking my photo of Ida Bell back where it belonged. Me and Lisbeth came upstairs a while ago to sleep a few winks before Ida Bell got here, but that was useless. We couldn't help but review each and every detail of the night the same way a mother studies every speck of her newly born baby.

Lisbeth came out from under her pillow. "Yeah, I sure did. I bet there was a photo album up under him, don't you think?" she said.

"I reckon so, or a journal, and he wrote in it before he . . . you know."

"Died?"

"Right." I didn't like that word. I never liked change at all, and somebody dying changes a whole heap of things.

"I think I'll sneak over there and poke around soon as they pull down the police tape," Lisbeth said. Mr. Whetstone's property was outlined by stretched out yellow tape that said "POLICE LINE DO NOT CROSS" in black over and over. "Momma said it'll come down today since they already know arson's not a factor."

"How do they know that?" I asked.

"Didn't you hear? The fire chief found a 'hot spot' where Mr. Whetstone left a candle burning all night long. That's what started this whole mess. He said it happens all the time, that it's a silent disaster needing way more attention than it gets. You know, Mr. Whetstone liked having himself a little candlelit prayer time each and every night."

Candles calmed my nerves. Ida Bell told me once that when I missed her at night, to light up a candle and I'd feel better. It worked, too. I guess Whet Whetstone didn't set his candle in a wide-mouth Mason jar like Ida Bell gave me. I decided to ask her for a different idea on giving me peace at night. I never wanted to see another burning candle, long as I lived.

I sat up in bed and leaned in toward Lisbeth. "I don't really think you need to go meddling around over there, Lisbeth. Daddy said Mr. Whetstone's house heated up to over a thousand degrees just minutes after the fire started. It's bound to still be hot. You could get burned."

Lisbeth disappeared back under her pillow. My fraidy-cat side got on her nerves. "I plan on being careful. It's interesting seeing what things look like all burned up." She had more nerve than Will, Meri, and me put together. I knew for a fact that nothing on God's green earth could make me set foot over there. Ever. She peeked out. "Besides, don't you want to find out more about the book Mr. Whetstone threw himself over?"

"Well, sure I do. I'm fixing to step downstairs and ask Momma if she knows. She hasn't left for work yet. Be right back." Momma had a way of finding out things nobody else could. I made it halfway down the stairs when her voice, barking at Daddy, reached me and stopped me dead.

Momma's wits were standing on their very end. "William, now, you know we can't keep on going like this. Daisy Street just isn't what it used to be. You got the Wadsworths next door. I like him fine, but she's nosier than a bloodhound and their boy must be trying to win some kind of Halloween contest with his looks and all. You got the Meadowbrook neighborhood through the woods with all sorts of meanness going on. And now this? I do *not* want to live next to the eyesore of a burned down house, especially one where all folks are gonna think of is a person dying. Truth is, William, I don't want to live in Monroe County anymore. I need something entirely different."

I held my breath for fear its sound would drown out Momma's words. While she talked about moving, my head stuffed up with cotton. The baluster I steadied myself on gave way, coming unattached from the staircase handrail. I stuck it back where it belonged. No matter how fancy a place is, if a person looked hard enough, the coming-apart pieces sure enough showed up.

"I know, Sadie, I know. We could look into buying a piece

of land on the outskirts of the county and building a new house. Get a little further away from town and all the people you deal with at work," Daddy said, and I let out my breath. Please, Momma, please listen to him. Momma and Daddy had thought about moving to a new neighborhood for a while now, which I could handle. I knew I'd keep in touch with Harper, but I couldn't bear the thought of moving so far away that Ida Bell and me wouldn't see each other every day. Just thinking of it felt like getting buried alive.

Momma started in again. "I'd really like to just begin again someplace new. Get out of Monroe County, maybe earn my social work Master's and work in a hospital in a bigger town. I want to stop going into folk's homes where I see lives torn up like Will's blue jeans."

My eyes dried up on account I hadn't blinked in a while. *Someplace new…begin again.* Fear crept up my back and sat down on my shoulders. All I wanted in the whole wide world was for Ida Bell to live in shouting distance. Momma and Daddy stopped talking when Ida Bell creaked open the screen door.

"Miz Callaway? What in the world done happened next door?" Ida Bell asked. Before Momma could answer, Ida Bell added, "Now, where Gracie-girl at?"

That gave me a smile, her asking about me right off like that.

"She's upstairs resting a little bit. We've been up since three o'clock in the morning, Ida Bell. Whet's house caught fire in the night, and we were sure ours was next with the wind blowing flames like you would not believe. If the good Lord wasn't with us . . ." Momma said through a tissue.

I couldn't sit there any longer. "Ida Bell!" I said, skipping as many steps as possible to get to her. I jumped into her arms like I was five years old again, and then out of nowhere my face was full-up with tears. Ida Bell was warm and her love poured into me and kept me standing. My tears poured onto her, and she stood there strong enough for me, her, and the mess I was making.

"Well, now, Gracie-girl, I suppose you right tired. Let me get a good look at you," she said, brushing my hair out of my face with one hand and not letting go of me with the other. "Sounds like some kind of morning you done had!" Ida Bell always managed a smile, and I was never far behind.

I caught my breath and stared into her deep eyes, brown and flowy and soft like the waters of the Alabama River. "Can we walk down to the berry patch, Ida Bell?" I said. After holding on to all that the fear during the fire, after knowing Mr. Whetstone was gone, and after letting out my cries on Ida Bell, I was all washed out. My arms didn't want to lift, and my legs didn't want to carry me anywhere except someplace worry-free.

"Gracie-girl, you reading my mind! That do sound mighty fine. And when we get back, we gone wash up our berries and smother 'em in cream. Maybe since you done had a trouble-some morning, we'll sprinkle ourselves a little sugar on the top, too," she said with a spark.

The heaviness of all I'd been through rose up off me a little. Having Ida Bell here was like coming up for air after being under water too long.

Momma picked up her purse and Daddy his briefcase. Momma went on out the back to the garage, but Daddy stepped out to the front foyer and stared over toward next door. He looked back at me, sadness wrapped up in his eyes, and quoted,

> *Ev'n from the tomb the voice of nature cries*

and I went on to finish,

> *Ev'n in our ashes live their wonted fires*

The heavy words pressed down on my middle like someone else's hands resting on my hips. He and Momma went on their way to work while Ida Bell and me went ours. It was sure enough strange how a day carried on as usual in spite of a whole house and a whole person being gone.

7

IDA BELL and me punched holes in the sides of two empty coffee cans so we could tie strings to them. We hung the cans around our necks to free up our hands for berry-picking. I reckon we looked right funny in our berrying clothes, the kind that don't mind getting torn here and there by briars. She took my hand, and we headed out. Her hand nestled just right around mine. I guess some things were meant to go together, like a great big front porch and rocking chairs filled up with friends.

When we opened the front door, the outside air hit me with the stench of a bad memory. It hung there—the choking smoke smell trapped in the steam of morning. As the sun streamed in from the south, leftover water vapor from the fire hoses rose, and Mr. Whetstone's place looked like a lake covered in early fog. "Ida Bell, I don't want to see that burned up stuff anymore. Can we just walk on down the road?" I asked.

"All right, then, Gracie-girl."

Just like always, Ida Bell danced down Daisy Street heel-and-toe style like the famous vaudeville tap dancer, Bojangles. I couldn't help but get happy with her. In spite of it all, I was ready for a break from hanging like a storm cloud. "Honey child, they's times you gots to laugh to keep from crying!" she said. Ida Bell hummed the "Maple Leaf Rag" and let her arms and legs swing and sway as they pleased. I loosened up, too, and moved to Ida Bell's rhythms.

"Uh-oh, Ida Bell, there's that nosy Miz Wadsworth watching us out of her window. See how the curtain's pulled to the side just enough? She'll talk about you and me all over town. I can just hear it now, 'Those two have no respect for what's happened, dancing up and down the street before God and everybody else.'"

"Now then, Gracie, you know fretting over what other folks gone think and say sort of makes you their slave. And child, that slavery done run its course!" she said with an I-mean-it accent. Then she danced with even more energy. Ida Bell's feet tapped in inventive and expressive moves I'd never in my life seen before. Whatever Miz Wadsworth thought or said, Ida Bell's dancing was mighty fine.

The blackberries grew at the end of Daisy Street just after the Wadsworth place. I was glad Ida Bell and me were together because I didn't want to run into Rebel Wadsworth all by myself. He was only three years older than me, but he made me want to turn and run every time I saw him. I swear that boy had nails in his heart and Tabasco sauce in his brain. He came from good people, so nobody really knew how he turned out so poor. Momma said just because a cat has kittens in the oven, don't mean they're gone rise like biscuits. Nobody even knew Rebel's real name. If a person tried to call him anything else, Rebel said he'd knock them so hard they'd see tomorrow.

No sign of him this morning, so my dancing loosened up a little more. The scent of seasoned berries and pinesap warming under the sun in the piney woods hit my nose and I had the feeling of getting close to home after a long time away.

When Ida Bell and me came to the berry patch, nobody else was allowed besides me and her. No brother, no sisters; shoot, we didn't even bring any of the dogs along. Just us. The only distractions were sweet berries, whistling birds, and good climbing trees. I reckoned I could handle that all right.

"Shoo-wee, Ida Bell, I need me some toothpicks to hold my eyes open!" I said. With that just-right slant of morning sunshine warming me up, all I wanted to do was find a good laying-down spot.

"I don't see no reason why you can't just let your eyes go on and close a spell. You was up before the birds this morning." Ida Bell sat down under a nearby pine. She studied the spot real careful-like to see that there was no poison ivy creeping up that tree. Wild blackberries and poison ivy sure liked each other's company. "Come on over here, Gracie-girl."

I curled up next to her and rested my head in her lap, studying the red and blue patchwork on her berry-picking pants. I let out a little giggle at the sight of us in clothes God wouldn't put on a billy goat, and so did she. For once, the hum of mosquitoes lulled me like a for-real lullaby. The katydids singing from the treetops added harmony, and it never felt better in all my life to let my eyes seesaw shut. Ida Bell fanned us both to keep the biting bugs at bay, and added her own music to the outdoor orchestra. She sang "This Little Light of Mine," and I don't even remember the last "let it shine" before I was gone.

🌿 8 🌿

I JUST kept my eyes closed when I woke up, kept on breathing heavy, and kept still like the thick air around us. I wasn't ready to give up this goodness. Ida Bell was still, too, and I thought maybe she'd dozed off with me until her familiar humming of "Swing Low, Sweet Chariot" let me know different. We always sang jubilee songs in the berry patch. "Swing Low" was my favorite because we sang it together as a proper call and response chant. She sang the leading lines and I followed with "Coming for to carry me home." When the time was right, I came in with my part, which got us both up and moving about again.

Ida Bell reached for our coffee cans. "Now, Gracie, leave them berries be if they green or red. You just worry about them plump, shiny black ones that want to fall off the vine nice and easy-like."

I liked the feel of those night-colored berries in my hands, all squishy, soft and firm at the same time. They smelled as fresh as the farmers market before the crowds arrived.

"Ain't they shiny, honey-child?" Ida Bell said, her face framed in golden light. What shined was her, and I wondered if she had any idea at all how much I loved her.

That got me to remembering. "Ida Bell, when you got here this morning, Momma and Daddy were talking about packing up and moving someplace new."

"Was they, now?"

"After the fire, Momma slumped down into one of her sinking spells, and started in on how she needs a different place to work, different place to live. Said she's good and tired of Monroe County."

"Well, now, we all gets tired of Monroe County every now and then. You move someplace new, you gone get tired of it too, every now and then."

"She's more than tired, though. She wants to leave, and she's serious about it."

"Now, how's this different from the last time she up and wanted to move?"

I sat my can down so I could look at Ida Bell. "For Momma, there's just not enough right, and too much wrong about staying. Work weighs her down, the neighborhood next to ours took a turn downhill, and our Daisy Street neighbors—well, on one side you got a kid who's got horns like the devil—and on the other you got a leftover fire and the memory of somebody dying. Put it all together and it means Momma wanting to get the heck outta here and never looking back."

"Mmm-hmm, I see what you saying."

"But, Ida Bell, what about you and me?"

"Now, I knowed you was thinking that." She put her can down, too. "Gracie-girl, you-and-me always gone be you-and-me. Ain't no new place can take that."

I buried my face in her side, and all our arms wrapped around each other. I wanted to cry, but when Ida Bell said, "Let's us not worry about all this till they's something concrete to go on," I choked on my tears for her sake. Ida Bell took my crying more serious than anybody. Most times when I cried, she did, too. She handed me my coffee can. With our backs bent beneath the watery sunshine, I hummed along to Ida Bell's jubilee songs. When we had enough blackberries for both our families to bake cobblers, plus some left over for the two of us to eat with cream, we headed out toward home.

Ida Bell and me held our hands out into the light to see who's were stained the purplest. On the backsides, mine were way more purple. Either that, or the purple just showed up more. What was funny, though, was that our skin was darn near the same color on our palms, with or without berry stains. Hers were darker in the creases.

Now, I don't know the slightest bit about palm reading on account of my Daddy serving as a part-time preacher and all, but the lines on Ida Bell's hands were long and dark and deep. I figured that meant she had an awful lot of love and life in her. While we held our hands to the light, all her palm lines pointed straight at me, and all mine straight at her. I knew deep down that Ida Bell and me were blood related somehow, someway. Plus, she and Momma both had the last name of "Lee" before Momma married Daddy, so I knew for sure and certain that if I could look way, way, way, way back in the family tree records, I'd find just exactly how she was my kin.

Through our fingers, I caught sight of folks coming down Daisy Street. "Look a-there, Ida Bell. It's Rebel Wadsworth and Blake Cooley, headed straight for us like arrows to a target. Looks like they've got something important to tell us."

"Well, it'd be the first time I ever heard something important come from Mr. Wadsworth's mouth," she said, giving us both a giggle. Ida Bell rarely talked about a soul, so when she did, it stood out and folks tended to listen. I liked it that she refused to call him "Rebel." She said making folks call you something that ain't your name is a way of bullying other people, and she was having none of it.

Now, Blake Cooley constituted a whole different story. The only person I knew besides Ida Bell not scared of Rebel? Blake Cooley. Lord knows I tried to be friends with Blake. We sure were different, though. I swear the boy looked like he was raised on red JELL-O. There's just no color to him but shades of red dirt in front of his sunken eyes. Plus, he's missing his two front teeth on the top. Daddy said when he sees Blake give a grin, he don't know whether to smile back or kick a field goal. Blake Cooley always asked me if I wanted to ride over to his house for some pickle toast, whatever God-forsaken concoction that was. At least it wasn't JELL-O, though. Maybe if Blake wasn't always squishing one of his earlobes up into his ear, I might have considered trying pickle toast.

Blake rode over here, always barefoot, from the "other" neighborhood through the path in the woods. Momma

didn't allow me over in Meadowbrook. She said shame happened over there, and that a child could easily get snatched
up and never heard from again. I snuck over there through
the sewer tunnel one time, and didn't see any shame. The
houses sat closer together than they did in my neighborhood, and most of the swimming pools were the plastic,
above ground kind. The chained up dogs knotted up my
stomach, though; looked like they'd just as soon have a
chunk of my leg than a store-bought bone. For some reason, Blake always rode up and down Daisy Street instead of
Macon Drive where his house was.

"A fine day to you boys," Ida Bell called as Rebel and Blake
quickened their pace to a run toward us.

"Y'all better get on inside! Didn't you hear?" They were
both screaming their heads off like the rapture had happened
and we were left over. Ida Bell and me traded glances, and
waited to see what Rebel and Blake were carrying on about.

9

"Now, what you boys going on so about?" Ida Bell said, unimpressed with Rebel and Blake's hoopla. Blake looked at Rebel, who spoke up first. "The Whetstone place is haunted now, and it ain't just any old ghost, either."

Then Blake chimed in, "Yeah, I done seen it with my own two eyes. It's preachy-kinda haunted. I seen that Whetstone man pacing back and forth with his Bible like he was behind the pulpit or something."

"I saw it, too," Rebel said, shaking his head as if Blake needed validation. "They said Whet Whetstone was dead, but we heard his very own voice chattering away about fire and brimstone and burning forever and ever."

Ida Bell shot a look at me, and me at her, both our eyebrows raised in question. "Now, you boys know people gone talk after something like this happens. We gots to keep our heads about us, though," Ida Bell said. "Come on now, Gracie, let's us get these berries on home."

"But that ain't all, y'all," Blake said.

Ida Bell stopped walking, so I did, too.

Blake put his hands on his hips and raised up his eyebrows. "If you carry the Good Book up to where the front door used to stand, the wind stirs up, flips your Bible open, and then your eyes land square on the verse you're meant to read," he said.

"Sure enough does," Rebel said.

"Rebel Wadsworth, I know you don't own a single Bible, so how would you know?" I asked.

"Blake here found one laying in Mr. Whetstone's yard. Must've been the book the fire chief said Mr. Whetstone was curled up over when he died. We was just messing around, sifting through the Bible to try and figure out why he wanted to save it so bad, but when we got to the old front door, it all happened just like Blake said."

"You mean to tell me that Wheaton Whetstone's Bible opened up to something you were *supposed* to read?" I asked.

"Dang straight it did," Rebel said, hands perched on his hips.

"Well, now, what it said?" Ida Bell asked, serious as a tornado warning. Ida Bell never poked fun when kids were earnest about something, even if it had a made-up feel to it.

"We think them words was for Rebel here," Blake said. "They said something about sending fire to the earth, and how that fire ought to already be lit. Anybody can see a finger was pointing to Rebel and how he ain't right with the Lord. I reckon Mr. Whetstone's fire happened to catch Rebel's attention."

Rebel rolled his eyes and then shot a stern look toward Blake. "Now, don't go spouting off too much about all this, or carrying it too far," he said. "Only reason I'll even think on it is because them words was spoken by the Lord Jesus Himself."

"Now, you mean to tell me that Jesus Christ talked straight to you, as in *personally?*" I asked, giving Rebel my best "get real" look.

Blake came to Rebel's defense. "Them words we read in the Good Book? They was written in red letters. They was said by Jesus, and everybody knows that the words of Jesus endureth forever, so it don't matter when he said them. They was meant for Rebel here."

"Now, what makes you think that Bible opening wasn't no one-time kind of thing?" Ida Bell said.

"'Cause we tried it again, and Blake got himself a verse, too," Rebel said. "Blake ain't never had more than two nickels clanging around in his pocket. His family can't even fix his teeth so he can eat right. Listen to what his verse said…"

Blake interrupted. "Hold on, I wrote it down." He reached into his back blue jean pocket and pulled out an old burger wrapper he'd written on. "Listen here,

For you know the grace of our Lord Jesus Christ, that though
He was rich, yet for your sakes He became poor, that you
through His poverty might become rich
Now, if that ain't about me, I don't know what is.

"How you figure that's about you, now, Blake?" Ida Bell said.

"'Cause why don't I have no money, when all these rich folks just through the woods got more than they need? It ain't right, and I finally got my reason for it. I'm poor on account that's gone help somebody someday. I just don't know who yet is all."

"Mmm-hmm," Ida Bell said, looking gently at Blake. "I imagine you right. Well, thank you boys. We appreciate you telling us. We best get on home, now."

Rebel and Blake disappeared into the woods, their arms flailing as they relived the scene at Whet Whetstone's all over again. Ida Bell and me made our way on home.

❦ 10 ❦

"IDA BELL, you think Rebel's gonna change on account of that Bible verse about fire?"

"Well, now, we can hope, can't we? He ain't bad as he seems, though. Just going through a little spell, I imagine."

"You think those verses stand for something, I mean *for real?*"

"I reckon that depends on who reads them, Gracie. If a person wants to believe them—well, that's they business."

"What if it's like horoscopes? Momma says no matter whose horoscope you read, you can imagine it being written for your own self. Says it could just as well be written for your pet dog."

Ida Bell giggled while she opened the front door. "Gracie-girl, you a mess! How 'bout some blackberries and cream?"

"I'll get them washed up!" I gently held the berries, one handful at a time, and let the cleansing water shine them up and run on through my fingers. The berries were all polishy, like the ones in the watercolor Ida Bell painted for me when I was little. My mind got to thinking again about leaving her and moving to some useless new place that Momma'd eventually get tired of. I got situated beside Ida Bell at our table instead of sitting across from her like usual. I turned our chairs so they faced each other because I wanted to see all of her at one time. I didn't want to miss out on one speck of her goodness.

"Now, Gracie-girl, you just keep on letting them berries fill up your bowl till at least two or three falls out to the table. That way, you know you gots enough," Ida Bell said with a wink.

Then came the cream, silky-smooth like Momma's perfectly laundered Sunday dresses. We sprinkled sugar on top and watched it sparkle until it disappeared. Our bowls looked so beautiful, we just stared. Purples, ebonies, and creamy ivories swirled around like a blackberry rainbow. I had the urge to rub the berry soup all over my face and arms and legs.

Ida Bell shut her eyes and pushed her lips together like she was letting the taste sink down into her bones. "Now, why don't we enjoy this nice and quiet-like," she said. "Seems like we done passed through a whole day, but that morning sun still rising! Ain't no use messing up this berry goodness with chatter. If you gots something real important to say, though, just go on and say it." We ate one berry at a time, drawing out the calm, basking in the sweetness.

"Ida Bell?" Momma called, and I took note that the clock didn't show lunch break time just yet.

"We in here, Miz Callaway. Come on in and get some fresh berries!"

"Why, thank you, Ida Bell. I'm so hungry my sides are caving in! But I can't stay. I've got to visit a family today out in Burnt Corn, and I just came by for a quick minute. I want Grace to ride with me."

A flower bloomed in my heart thinking about having Momma all to myself for a while, even if it wouldn't exactly be fun.

"Can we stop by Mr. Twilly's place, Momma?" Mr. Twilly farmed corn and cotton, and for a little more money in his family's pocket he made and sold white oak baskets right off his front porch. He wove nesting baskets, round or square baskets with or without lids, and gizzard baskets, which he called the "Cadillac" on account they're hard to make and cost the most. Mr. Twilly wore a three-piece pinstriped suit every day of the world, even during the dog days of summer. "Gots to be looking fine for my clientele!" he'd say. He and Momma sure loved jawing at each other, and could carry on for hours at a time. I thought maybe stopping by to visit with him would remind Momma of all the good folks living around here, maybe get her mind off packing up for a better life.

"We'll see, Peamite. It depends on how long our work visit lasts," Momma said.

"You think we're gonna be gone a while? Want me to bring some books?" I asked. Usually on these trips with Momma, I ended up staring at the floor while she talked with people and wrote down what they said. It sometimes took a real long time. Momma didn't allow me to bring anything noisy, so I carried books with me. Even then, she instructed me to turn the pages real slow and quiet-like.

"No, Peamite. Best not to bring anything this time. It wouldn't be proper," she said.

I watched Momma pull her Colt revolver down from the top shelf of the walk-in pantry. I was, under no circumstance, ever allowed to touch that gun. Matter of fact, I wasn't allowed to touch the shelf it laid on. Momma held it, barrel facing the floor, and loaded six bullets into the cylinder. She lowered it into her purse, letting the handle stay slightly visible. I looked to Ida Bell for an explanation, but she shrugged her shoulders.

Ida Bell gave me a good hug. "Now, Gracie-girl I won't be seeing you for a few days, you hear?"

"Why's that?" I asked.

"I gots to drive down to Mobile tomorrow and Friday, and then we'll be on into the weekend. Be seeing you bright and early Monday morning. You rest up tonight, now, you hear? You done been through an ordeal."

No Ida Bell tomorrow? I disguised my disapproval under a cordial little smile and hugged her back. Didn't matter how much I smiled, though. Ida Bell knew me like a person knows their own secrets.

"Bye-bye, Ida Bell," Momma said. "We'll see you soon. Peamite, run a comb through your hair and get your sandals on, then meet me at the VW."

"What do you need that gun for, Momma?"

"I'll explain on the way. We can't get there late."

11

Momma and me loaded ourselves into our tan 1964 Volkswagen Bug and rolled the windows down right off. Momma said we shouldn't ride in a fancy car around folks who can't afford any kind of car at all. Wouldn't be proper. This car, that gun, and Momma's telling me not to bring anything had me sweating like a pitcher of iced tea out on the porch. Momma eased her loaded purse between her left leg and the driver's side door. She checked to see that the gun handle sat at a quick reach.

"Gracie, got your seatbelt on? Do NOT touch my purse. Make sure your knee doesn't hit the shift knob. This thing pops in and out of gear if you just look at it cross-eyed. Is your door locked?" she asked. Momma always said if something were to go wrong, at least she'd know she'd done her best to prevent it. She wasn't even looking to see that I was listening, just going about her quiz ritual.

"Momma, you've gotta tell me about that gun sitting

there on the floorboard. Are we going someplace dangerous?"
I asked.

Momma shifted the Bug into reverse and we backed out
of the garage. She steadied her purse before shifting into
first. "Peamite, it's not so much the place that's dangerous.
The couple we're going to visit, Layla and Bobby Ray, are at
rock bottom, and sometimes deep sadness can come out like
anger."

I wasn't so sure now that I wanted to ride out there with
Momma, and I wondered if it was a good idea for her to be
heading out to the sticks where somebody might get angry at
her, whether it was on account of sadness or not. "Are they in
trouble over their kids?" I asked.

"No, sweetie. They're good, loving parents. But their
two-month-old baby daughter died in her sleep night before
last, and they don't have any money for a burial. They need
my help."

I'd never met these folks Momma was talking about, but
right off I wanted to hide my head in my hands. My insides
hollowed out, like I was about to float up to the clouds. I could
barely think about a little baby girl dying. It was like somebody turned the lights out on my mind. A thought would
almost come to me, and then nothing but the world spinning
by. Out the window, tiny pink things all over the place seemed
to have a spotlight shining on them. Roadside flowers. Pink
bottles hanging in somebody's tree to ward off evil. Bubble
gum wrappers sticking out of the ashtray. Everywhere, little
splashes of baby girl pink.

"How are you gonna help Layla and Bobby Ray, Momma?"

"I don't know just yet, Peamite. I need to see them, see the baby, and then ask what they need."

A gasp collected in my throat. "See the baby? The baby's gonna be where we're going?" I asked, thinking I might have misunderstood.

"She is, Peamite, and there's not a thing in the world to be scared of. Death is just as perfectly natural as life." Momma said.

"But what will she look like?"

"Like a resting baby, sweetheart. Layla and Bobby Ray have two other children, and I want you to talk to them, okay? I imagine they'd enjoy having a friend right about now."

"Okay, Momma. I will." I wondered if I'd ever been asked to do something this hard before, this important. What if I didn't know what to say? What not to say? Whether to hold my hands neatly in front of me or keep them still inside my pockets? What if I made things worse on those kids?

❦ 12 ❦

AFTER a tangle of red dirt roads, I was completely turned around. Momma knew these Alabama back roads like her own history. The farther into the country we drove, the poorer the world turned. Houses hung together like old skeletons. Rooftops caved in, old wooden house frames stood without a drop of paint on them, fence boards hung by rusty nails; if I hadn't known better, I would've thought this to be a ghost town. These near dead houses stood lonely, and yet, some were lovely. I especially liked the one completely covered in kudzu. The big green leaves climbed their way clear to the top and coiled 'round and 'round, looking like a giant leafy snake. Only way I could tell somebody lived in there was that the kudzu'd been cut away from the front door.

"These poor folks, Grace. They've got hungry chickens and hungrier children galore. They've got piles of red dirt and swamps full of poison ivy and snakes. Come to think of it, they've got everything but jobs and a way out," Momma said, her heart full for them.

"How do you get this poor, Momma?"

"You don't *get* this poor, Peamite; you're born poor and what you *get* is poorer."

Momma stopped the VW in front of a ramshackle trailer. Toys scattered the yard, and pink, leftover azalea blossoms parched from too much sun and too little water hung from stems like old balloons from a party. Chickens scratched at the ground, looking for anything but dirt. The trailer looked like it had just blown there during a tornado from somewhere else. It didn't sit up on blocks, or up on anything. Pieces of its sides hung limp, not holding together anymore.

"Now, Grace, be on your best behavior. These folks are going through a tough time. Show them how polite you can be."

"Yes, ma'am."

Momma slid her purse strap over her shoulder, and made sure that the barrel of that gun pointed down and that the handle showed slightly. Chickens scattered as we waded through them. There was no front door on the trailer, but a moth-eaten bed sheet nailed to the doorframe instead. The sheet had tiny pink rosebuds all over it, and I thought again of the still little baby girl on the other side.

Momma knocked on the doorframe. "Layla, Bobby Ray? It's Sadie Callaway. Y'all getting along all right?" Momma called.

A young lady, too young for the sorrow draped around her shoulders, pushed the sheet to one side. Her eyes were all puffy and sore-looking. Past the sadness in her eyes, there was deep, stormy blue, but it was darn near impossible to see deeper than the sad shadows.

"Miz Callaway, thanks so much for coming. We didn't know who else to call," she said, drying her eyes on her sleeve. The sight of Momma broke her, as if she'd been waiting all her life for someone to give her a smile.

"Well, I'm so glad you did call," Momma said. "We'll get this all figured out, don't you worry a single bit." Momma put her arms around Layla and stroked her back. "Layla, this is my Gracie. She wanted to say hey to your two older children, if you don't mind."

Layla looked at me like it hurt even to move her eyes from Momma over to me. "Gracie. That's a right pretty name. Come on in, sugar," Layla said.

She guided us through the particleboard entryway and into the only room there was. The smell reminded me of a field trip my fourth grade class took to the Monroe County Sawmill. There was no proper floor in there, but just the same red dirt as the road outside, and two girls younger than me sat real quiet-like in a corner, playing jacks best they could in the dirt.

"Girls, this here's Gracie, Miz Callaway's youngun. Y'all play nice now while I talk with her momma," Layla said.

I wondered if Momma or Layla or Bobby Ray could hear my heart thumping. I'd never in my life trembled in fear before now. I gave a weak "Hey, y'all," my words coming out all trembly, and sat beside them in the dirt.

"Them's sure are pretty bow ribbons in your hair," the littlest one said to me, handing me a super-ball.

Right off, my cheeks turned red at having something they didn't. "Thank you," I said, and bounced the ball hard so it wouldn't stall in the dirt.

"Layla, may I see your little angel?" Momma asked.

Layla held her arm up in the direction of the baby. Her lips pushed together, like there were thoughts in her mind that she wouldn't set free as words. Momma motioned for me to get up off the floor and follow her.

Right there in the middle of all this dirt, all this hurt and poor, was the most beautiful thing I'd ever laid eyes on. There was a pure white bassinet with a pink gingham ribbon curling down from the hood and a lacy skirt all around. Inside, it held a tiny baby with her eyes closed. She wore a soft nightgown the color of a faded valentine, and her arms cuddled a little teddy bear that would play music.

"Just look at that. She's as pretty as roses covered in morning dewdrops. Pure peace itself," Momma said to Layla. She took a tissue from her purse and pushed that gun out of sight. She must've been convinced that their hurt wouldn't come out angry-like. Momma put her hands on the baby's chubby little cheeks and looked deeply at her.

"She's with God. At least I'm sure of that," Layla said to Momma.

"And so are you, Layla, right here and now," Momma said.

"Then, I guess in a way, we're still together."

"I'm sure of that," Momma said.

Layla looked at Momma, her heart broken but having to beat nonetheless. "Miz Callaway, we don't have no money for a service. The ladies at the church brought this here bassinet. We can't afford a casket, neither. I'm so scared. My baby girl has died, and the only thing worse than that is not knowing when her death will come to an end, what with her laid out in the house like this and all," Layla said, looking over at Bobby Ray who'd been so silent I'd forgotten he was sitting there on the sofa. He was still, and blended in with the blandly colored couch. His eyes were empty, and he stared at the dirt that was their floor. If I didn't know better, I'd have thought he didn't know he was in the world. "She deserves a proper burial, and the girls need that too, to finish this. I can't bear this endlessness."

"Now, you don't worry about one single thing," Momma said. "I'm driving straight from here to the funeral home out near my place. I'll arrange a service and casket for your sweet angel. I'll stop back by in the morning to see if the plan works for you."

"Well, I just don't know how I could ever thank you, Miz Callaway," Layla said, breathing what looked like the deepest breath she'd taken in days.

"Gracie, say goodbye to these sweet girls," Momma said.

"It was nice to meet y'all," I said, and handed them each a pink ribbon from my hair. They looked over at Layla, question marks in their eyes, little grins on their mouths.

"Go on and take them, girls. It ain't proper to refuse a gift," Layla said.

Momma and me ducked back under the rosebud sheet and made our way to the VW. After all this, I wondered how long it would be before Momma disappeared on me down into that dark space of hers.

❧ 13 ❧

I WAS covered in red dirt, and Momma frowned on account I tracked it all inside the VW. It stained my sandals, my legs, and I must've breathed so much of it in that my thoughts turned to red mud puddles, too. "Momma, what are they gonna do with that little baby?"

"They're going to bury her, Peamite."

"But she's so new. A little tiny thing like that shouldn't be all by herself down in the dirt, Momma. How will her momma and daddy and sisters ever let go of her?" My mouth turned down and I squeezed my eyes shut. The tears water-falled over my cheeks and fell all over the rest of me, streaking my dirt-covered arms and legs.

"They won't let go of her, Gracie. They'll bury her, but they'll hold that angel baby the rest of their lives in their hearts."

Momma handed me a tissue. "Dry up, sweetie. We've got time to stop by Mr. Twilly's, and we'll be there in just a minute. Why don't we ask him to make us a basket you can give

Layla and Bobby Ray's girls? We'll fill it up with surprises to help them get through the next few days."

"That'd be real nice, Momma. Can we put a little something in there for Layla and Bobby Ray, too?"

"Well, how very sweet, Gracie," Momma said. She lifted her right hand off the steering wheel to pat my dirty leg, something my momma just didn't do while driving. Her love towards me sent me into an even deeper cry. When I saw Mr. Twilly's place, I had to hold my breath to stop my tears. It took three tissues to dry up my eyes, nose, face, and the rest of me. If there was anybody in this whole wide world besides Ida Bell and my daddy who could cheer me up, though, it was Mr. Twilly, the basket man.

We found Mr. Twilly same as always on his front porch in his pinstripes. He said he was first and foremost a farmer, but there wasn't a time I could remember stopping by that he wasn't sitting here with oak weaver in his hands, the long strips from the heart of a white oak tree taking on the shape of a basket.

"Well, now, ain't you two a sight! Come on up here to the porch and let me hug your neck, Gracie!" Mr. Twilly said.

I hopped up the red brick steps and wound my way around his half-made baskets. Mr. Twilly gave me a squeeze, and then studied my face. "Now, I ain't never seen nothing but a smile stretched across this youngun's face. Somebody go and pinch this child, Miz Callaway?"

"We've just come from Layla and Bobby Ray's, Mr. Twilly. You know them?" Momma asked.

"Sure I do," he said, shaking his head and then resting his chin in his hands. "Sure I do," he said a little quieter, looking down and shuffling scraps of heartwood from one place to another.

"Well, now, I thinks we could use us some of my world-famous Twilly-made lemonade," he said, the smile coming back to his eyes, and waved me to follow him out back. We pulled an armload of lemons off the only lemon tree I'd ever seen in my life, so bright they made the sun seem tucked under a cloud. Mr. Twilly grew his trees in huge baskets he made himself so he could move them inside during winter. We juiced the lemons, letting the liquid fall into a glass pitcher, stirred in some cane sugar, and then Mr. Twilly said, "Now, let me go fetch some ice from the ice box. It ain't lemonade unless it's so cold you almost can't drink it!"

While Mr. Twilly went after ice, I walked back to the porch and Momma and me looked through his baskets. We set a few aside to pick from for Layla, Bobby Ray, and the girls. Mr. Twilly's sunshiny voice got to us before he did, "Mmm-mmm, this here's sure-enough lemonade, not that excuse-of-a-drink they tries to sell you at the super market!" He pulled up apple crates, one for Momma and one for me. "Now, let's us sit a spell." The first sip sent all our faces into wrinkles and eye squeezes, but it was some kind of tasty.

"How's your corn crop this summer, Mr. Twilly?" Momma asked.

"Coming right along. Right thirsty, though. We don't get some rain soon, it's all gone be parched. Now, that reminds me . . . you gots to try out this batch, Gracie." Mr. Twilly handed me a Mason jar full of still-warm, boiled peanuts. I peeled the shell off one with my teeth and spit it in the yard, which was the only time I was allowed to spit with Momma around. When it was me and Ida Bell, I could also spit rabbit tobacco. Momma for sure didn't know about that, though.

"Mr. Twilly, which one of these baskets would work best for Layla and them?" Momma asked, pointing to the ones we'd set aside.

"Oh, I gots just the perfect one for you right here." Mr. Twilly held up one of his "Cadillac" baskets. "Look here at where the handle's woven in place. That's a special 'God's Eye' pattern. Be nice if them folks was reminded that God is sure enough watching out for them." Now that I looked for it, a lot of Mr. Twilly's baskets had the "God's Eye" pattern. It was shaped like a diamond on both sides of the handle.

"Well, Mr. Twilly, I can't think of anything nicer," Momma said, reaching for her wallet.

"Now, I can't charge you for this one, Miz Callaway. And there won't be any fussing on the matter," Mr. Twilly said.

"Well, that's fine of you. We'll fill it up real nice-like, and I know it'll make them smile."

"I sure do hope so. They's good folks. Right good folks," Mr. Twilly said.

Momma didn't jaw at him like usual, so I could tell her mind was still back at that dirt-floor trailer. She'd never in her life been so quiet on this particular front porch.

"Gracie, we best get going. Mr. Twilly, it was so wonderful seeing you."

I reached over and gave Mr. Twilly a hug. "Well, I sure thank you for that, young lady," he said.

"Thank you for the lemonade, Mr. Twilly. The basket, too. It's just right," I said.

"You mighty welcome. Y'all come see me again real soon, now, you hear?"

"We sure will," Momma said.

Momma and me loaded back up in the VW and rode on. Mr. Twilly sat there on his porch, his head in his hands like he was thinking on something real hard. I was thinking, too.

"Momma, when are you gonna die? And what about me? When will I die?"

14

MOMMA adjusted her seatbelt. She took her eyes off the winding, dusty road to look me in the eye. "Well, Peamite, I can't answer that in all honesty. I plan on living a real long time, time enough that you'll be all grown up and chasing your own children around. And you? My little Gracie—well, you just plan on living till you're old as Alabama red dirt. That's how it is with most everybody."

"Not for that little angel baby. And not for Mr. Whetstone, either."

"No, not for them. You're right. It's unusual how all this happened."

"Momma, I can't stop thinking about that baby. I've never, ever seen anything so pretty and peaceful. But she wasn't breathing! How can something fill up your heart and break it at the very same time?" I asked. The sting behind my nose meant tears were on their way.

Momma said, "That's love, sweetheart." That strong period at the end of her sentence meant she was done talking. She pulled away from me and went inside herself where I wasn't invited. I fisted my breath and held onto the tears that wanted out so I wouldn't frazzle Momma's nerves.

We turned onto Daisy Street. Everything swayed to its own rhythm, unaware of the shadow darkening my heart. The wildflowers bending in the breeze moved to music I couldn't hear. My world was falling quiet.

Momma nudged my arm as she parked the Bug. "Peamite, walk on down to the drugstore. They'll have plenty for our basket, and just ask Miz Calhoun to charge our tab. I'm fixing to head over to the funeral home. In the morning around eight o'clock, you and me'll ride back out to Layla and Bobby Ray's to see them again. I'm frying in here, so I'm just gonna make a quick switch over to the other car."

Momma smoothed her clothes, and got in her classic white Mercedes, turning the air on straight away. "When will you be back?" I asked.

"Oh, right soon. Probably by the time you get home. Now, run on."

I walked up Daisy Street as Momma's car got smaller and smaller up ahead. Why didn't she want me to go with her? And why didn't she want to go get the basket fixings together? She could've at least dropped me off by CK's Drugstore. She passed right straight by it on her way to the funeral home. Seemed like every day, Momma's heartplace drifted further and further away from mine.

I made it to the drugstore, and sat a spell in a rocking chair on the porch to cool off. This was the local spot where starch-shirted men and high-heeled women ordered "the usual, please" at the old-fashioned soda fountain. Folks came here to gossip, fill prescriptions, or just to pick up last-minute things on their way home. There were three aisles full of boring dishwashing detergent, shampoo, cough drops—that sort of thing. But aisle four looked like the manager spread a rainbow across the shelves. There was watermelon-flavored bubble gum, chocolate bars, shiny bags of chips, and coloring books that came with their own pack of sharpened crayons for little kids. Aisle four smelled like the air rising up around the cotton candy stand at the county fair.

My body was thick, like I'd been stuffed full of cinder blocks. It took some coaxing to get up out of that rocking chair and get on with my business. An air-conditioned wave breezed over me as I opened the drugstore door. I never could make it past Miz Mazie Calhoun. She'd worked behind the counter all my life. I never once saw her when she wasn't wearing a fancy hat, the spilly kind that blocks people's view at the picture show. And I never once saw her that she didn't try to get information out of me that we both knew was none of her business.

"Hey there, Miss Grace Callaway! How you doing, little lady?" Miz Calhoun asked with the extravagance of an opening circus act.

"I'm just fine, Miz Calhoun. How are you?"

"Oh, fair to middlin," she said, stepping out from behind the counter. I was in no mood to be quizzed by her, so I pretended not to notice she was coming and headed toward aisle four behind a shopping buggy. Nobody got away from Mazie

Calhoun, though. I soon felt her arm inching around my shoulders the way a skeleton's arm creeps around a person in a haunted house.

"Now, tell me, sweetheart. What happened over yonder at the Whetstone place?" As if I didn't already have enough burden scarved around my neck.

"Oh, they don't know just yet. I'll be sure to let you know if I hear anything. Excuse me, please," I said, wiggling out of her bony clenches and toward aisle four. "I've got to meet Momma back home in just a minute." I'd never had to cut loose from Miz Calhoun before on account Ida Bell always did it for me. Now, Momma, she'd answer more questions from Miz Calhoun than an information booth; but not Ida Bell. She'd have none of that, so I learned how to get away from Miz Calhoun from her.

Aisle four was exactly the right place to find surprises for those little girls back at the dirt-floor trailer. I found a four-pack of Play-Doh in red, yellow, blue and white, an etch-a-sketch, a lemon twist jump rope, Little Debbie Nutty Bars, Little Debbie Swiss Rolls, Little Debbie Fudge Brownies, and a lock and key journal. I put two of everything in my buggy.

Taking care to go the back way to avoid Miz Calhoun, I walked over to the gift section on aisle six to find something for Layla and Bobby Ray. They had the tiniest little silver angel pins, ones with golden halos and sparkling wings, and a little pink jewel where the heart is. They also had glassy rubbing stones, each one in its own velvet bag. Ida Bell brought me a stone smoothed by the Alabama River back when I was little and came down with the chicken pox, and I've been a stone-rubber ever since. I think part of the river gets inside the stone and forever runs clean and happy. Ida Bell said if I truly listened, I could hear the flowing waters in a river rock the same way ocean sounds can be heard in big seashells. I put two velvet bags and two angel pins down in my buggy.

I kept feeling like I wanted something that smelled good, too, so I walked to the candle display and picked one up with an "Eastern Red Cedar" scent. I couldn't put it down for sniffing as I walked up to the front.

"Did you find everything all right, little Miss Callaway?" Miz Calhoun asked.

"I sure did, all except for hair ribbons."

"Well, I imagine we could order you some. Tell me, now, what will you be needing them for?"

"Having three girls in one family, we go through a lot of ribbons." There was no way on this green earth I was getting into Layla and Bobby Ray's business with Mazie Information Calhoun. "Don't worry about ordering, though. I need them pretty fast. I'll just run down to the Tot Shop and pick some up."

"Well, all right, then. You sure do have an interesting assortment here. Are you having yourself a little party?"

"Yes, ma'am, I sure am. You have a nice evening, Miz Calhoun," I said, turning for the door.

"Tell your momma 'hey' for me! Do you need a ride? That's an awful lot for a girl little as you to carry!"

"No, ma'am, but I appreciate it," I said with a wave over my shoulder. Dadgumit if she wasn't right, though. This sack of surprises was making me walk lop-sided. I didn't care. Under no circumstances would I sit in a car with Mazie Calhoun while she fired question after question at me. I was a sopping wet mess by the time I reached Daisy Street, but I was too excited to care. I couldn't wait to show Momma our perfect basket stuffers, and wondered if she might want to ride back over to Layla and Bobby Ray's tonight instead of waiting all the way till morning.

❧ 15 ❧

OMMA'S Mercedes hummed into the garage, and I skipped through the kitchen to catch her. "Momma, wait till you see! It's perfect!" I yelled in her direction. Mr. Twilly's Cadillac basket sat all filled up and ready to go on the kitchen table. I ended up not needing to buy Tot Shop ribbons. There were enough extras in my ribbon box and in my sisters' drawers to outfit an entire Girl Scout troop. I tied them all around the handle and sides of Mr. Twilly's basket, all except for the "God's Eye" part, which I thought might not be proper to cover up.

Momma was still in the car, gathering up her work papers. "Momma! I found all kinds of things at the drugstore, but the part you're gonna like most is the ribbons. I've got polka dots, curly-Qs, bubble bows, saddle stitches, all kinds. Come on and see!"

Momma laid her work stack back down on the passenger's seat. She held the steering wheel with both hands and dropped her head. Her body rose, taking in a deep breath.

Use to be, Momma's face would light up just for seeing me excited. Not this time. I walked on out to the Mercedes to see about her.

"Momma? You want a hand with your work stuff?" Momma didn't raise her head. She held up her left hand in a "not now" wave. My body slumped, my spirits not far behind. If I left Momma alone like she was asking, I'd be doing just that: leaving her all alone. Even if that's what she wanted, it sure as heck wasn't what I wanted. If I stayed, I might make her feel even worse. This very thing terrified me, like walking a tightrope I knew dang well was fixing to snap. Every now and then, though, possibility outweighs fear.

I walked back into the kitchen and grabbed hold of the Cadillac basket. Didn't matter what kind of mood Momma was in, this basket was bound to give her a smile. Just the sight again of all that brightness, the sweet surprises, and Mr. Twilly's handiwork unslumped me, and a little giggle settled in my mouth. The lollipop ribbon colors were happy as a school playground. I reckon it was raining at recess time, though. Before I made it back to the garage, Momma dragged herself through the door and on past me and my basket like we weren't even there. "Momma, look here. Ain't it the prettiest thing you ever saw?"

"Peamite, I just can't," she said, so faint-like I wouldn't have known what she said if I hadn't heard it before.

Momma walked past the stairway and into the living room. She melted down into her rocking chair, no lamp on, and soaked tissue after tissue after tissue. A time or two she gasped for breath so hard I worried she might faint. I sat down on the stairs, curled up in a little ball. I was wanting to go sit with Momma, but I was afraid if I made things any worse, she might just die like Whet Whetstone and that beautiful angel baby. Seemed to me there wasn't much room left for getting worse.

I rested my chin on my knees and stayed put, needing to sit close to Momma without being in her way and on her nerves. I held my hand up to the wall and tried to feel her through it. Momma was right there on the other side of that wall that rose between us. Maybe she could feel me. Just maybe. My heart pounded so strong I could feel it against my curled up legs. My clothes were soaking wet. Momma'd just die if she knew I was wiping snot right on my sleeves, but I didn't care. I hugged my legs and pretended they were Momma, determined to be here for her, whether she knew it or not.

The long tunnel of oaks through the front door glass rested my eyes, my dizzy mind. Ida Bell says there's a reason we look out a window when we're indoors. Says we need to see bigger, wider than what's right in front of our eyes. Says we need to experience things too far away to see or hear right up close. There are voices way out there that don't use words. I stared into the far-off, listening.

Just then, Momma surprised me. She began playing "It is Well with My Soul" on the piano. Nothing else in this whole wide world sounded like my momma's hymn-playing. She knew when to grow loud or when to quiet the music, and her little tiny hands filled up more notes on a piano than seemed possible. She could turn one note into a thousand sounds. Momma's playing must have meant she was trying to make herself feel better, and I took that as a good sign.

She played the introduction, and I snuck down to the first step to peek around the wall. Her shoulders moved with the melody, anticipating the peace of the hymn as the song came forth. Momma went on into the first verse, playing just fast enough to gather the meaning of the words, but not so slow that the meaning was lost. With the pedal, she made the whole piece *legato*, and I swear angels could've sung to her accompaniment. Wanting her to know how beautiful her playing was, how beautiful *she* was while making angel music, I eased into the living room, sat down in one of the matching Victorian wing back chairs, and gave Momma a half-smile when she looked my way.

The very second Momma's gaze touched mine, the song that had so richly filled up the room and my heart, vanished. Instant silence. She was only halfway through the first verse. "Momma, play the rest. You can't stop in the middle, especially not the middle of *that* song."

"I just can't, Peamite. You go on, now, and see if your daddy's home yet."

"Yes, ma'am."

I did go on, but I did not see if Daddy'd come home. I sat back down on the stairs real quiet-like, hoping Momma'd get back on the piano without an audience. The only sounds coming from the living room, though, were fresh crying ones. When Daddy got home from work, he went straight to Momma like someone had told him she was in there. He picked her little body up and carried her directly to bed. In my imagination, the two of them became a fire fighter carrying Whet Whetstone from his house, weary, but breathing. When Daddy walked past me on the stairs, he whispered sweetly to her, "Sadie, darling, I don't know what Monroe County would do without you. This'll all be better in the morning." Daddy shot me a wink and a smile, and I knew he'd be back to see about me.

🌿 16 🌿

"GRACIE, did you hear the one about the nearsighted snake?" I rolled my eyes at hearing this for the fortyeleventh time. "He eloped with a rope!" Daddy said and eased down by me on the stairs.

"Sorry, Daddy. I'm not much in a laughing mood just now." Daddy shook his head like he understood. He took hold of my hand and quoted,

> Out of the night that covers me,
> Black as the pit from pole to pole

and then I came in,

> I thank whatever gods may be
> For my unconquerable soul

"Don't you worry about your momma, Gracie. She's the strongest lady I've ever known. She'll be raring to go first thing in the morning. Reach on down in my shirt pocket and see what's there." I dug around the pocket of Daddy's starched blue button-down and pulled out a pine straw bracelet, just my size. He'd been weaving these for me ever since I could remember. He tied it around my left wrist and gave my hand a kiss.

"Come on and help me get some supper on the table," Daddy said. "How about Shaggy Dogs this time?"

"All right, Daddy. I'll make your secret sauce, okay?"

"You just wish you knew the recipe!" Daddy always acted like his hot dog sauce was a take-to-your-grave secret. Everybody knew it was just plain old ketchup, mustard, and mayonnaise mixed together, equal parts. Tasted right good, though. These days, every time Momma skipped supper on account of crying, Daddy cooked up a fancy dog to get all us kids smiling. Now, he may not have been much of a cook, but one thing Daddy could do was dress a dog. He made Hot Dog Heaven Dogs that had so much cheese melted on top we ate them with our sleeves rolled up, Hot Diggety Dogs that were smothered in red hot chili, Hot Potato Dogs that had the fries inside the bun with the hot dog instead of on the side, The Dog with Two Tails that were topped with both a dill and a sweet pickle spear, the Dog Ate My Homework Dog that had alphabet pasta on top, Lucky Dogs that he served on Irish soda bread and always with hot tea, and Jimmy Carter Dogs that had peanut butter spread across the top.

We started pulling the fixings together for Shaggy Dogs and summer squash. Shaggy Dogs had shredded lettuce sticking out of the bun every which way. The squash came from Ida Bell's garden. Just boil and salt it, and that stuff tasted like a little piece of heaven. Daddy, determined to keep me in good spirits, was singing his own made-up verse to the tune of "Row, Row, Row Your Boat,"

I, I love my squash,
And my squash loves me.
A-meezy-meezy-meezy-squash and a-squashy-me

I set the table while Daddy made the sauce. He hid the ingredients like he could make millions if he'd only tell Betty Crocker. I made sure to get the table just right in case Momma came out for supper: napkins on the left with the fold-side out; knife on the right with its blade-side in; spoons, whether needed or not, to the right of the knife; forks to the left of the plate; water glasses at twelve o'clock above the plate; bread and butter plates above and slightly left of the forks.

"Y'all come on for supper!" Daddy called throughout the house. "Grace, go see if Momma won't come to the kitchen for supper, would you, please?"

"Yes, sir," I said, but kind of lingered on account I wasn't real comfortable heading toward Momma just now. Daddy must've noticed.

Presently my soul grew stronger
he quoted, and studied my face for assurance. I completed with,

Hesitating then no longer

I went on to Momma. I fingered the walls on the way, thinking of what I'd say if Momma was awake. I knocked real quiet-like in case she was resting, and eased open the bedroom door. Her eyes were closed but still blinking and her fingers tapped the sheets, so I knew she wasn't sleeping. "Momma?" I whispered, placing my hand on hers.

"Hi there, Peamite," she said, and pulled me up on the bed with her.

"Supper's ready, Momma. Daddy made his secret hot dog sauce."

"I don't think I can eat one more of those things," she said, hinting a smile. "Let me just sit here with you for a minute, lovebug." Momma ran her fingers through my hair, then held on to me like I was life itself. A tear ran down my cheek, but I didn't know if it was mine or hers. "We better get to the table," she said with a kiss to my forehead. "They'll all be waiting on us."

Picking up a fork before the host or hostess picked up theirs was given a stern stare at the Callaway table, part of what Momma called Proper Etiquette. Truth was, we were never to begin before Momma, even though Daddy usually did the hosting. If one of us blinked funny nowadays it sent Momma into feeling poorly, so we all aimed to get the Proper Etiquette rules just right. Will, Meri, and Lisbeth just sort of buried their heads in their Shaggy Dogs, not saying too much of anything. I was particularly bound and determined not to send Momma off to her sad place . . .

again. This wasn't real easy as Proper Etiquette was right involved:

1. Napkins stayed in laps and were *never* used for nose-wiping.
2. Elbows off the table!
3. Utensils were not to touch the table again once picked up.
4. Food was passed left to right.
5. Food was never reached for across the table.
6. Salt and pepper were passed together, even if only one was requested.
7. Passed dishes were placed on the table, not in a person's hands.
8. Hot food was not blown on for cooling-off purposes.
9. No talking with our mouths full, unless the rap-ture'd come.
10. No cutting more than two bites of food at a time.
11. Left hands were kept in your lap at all times, ex-cept for when you were using your knife.
12. No nose-blowing at the table. No exceptions!
13. Never use a toothpick. Ever.
14. Never announce that you need to use the restroom. Just say, "Excuse me, please."
15. When the meal was complete, silverware was placed diagonally across the plate.

Trying to remember all this was like counting ants in a kicked-over ant bed. I didn't usually have to give it much thought to get it right; but, under pressure, easy becomes hard. "Excuse me, please," I said, placing my napkin, unfolded but not wadded, to the right of my dinner plate. I opted for hunger over setting Momma off. I climbed the stairs, got into my polka-dotted jammies, and crawled into bed. I ran my fingers over the picture of Ida Bell under my pillow and thought how long today had been without her, how stretched-out the next three days would be without her. Sleep was the only thing that would make Monday morning get here faster when I'd see Ida Bell, and make tomorrow get here faster when Momma and me could carry our basket over to Layla and Bobby Ray's. Like Daddy said, Momma'd be her old self in the morning.

🌿 17 🌿

"PEAMITE, you 'bout ready to go?" Momma called from the hallway. The clock read 6:45 A.M.

"Yes, ma'am," I half-whispered, trying not to wake up Lisbeth. Didn't matter what time Momma said we needed to leave for any place, she was waiting with her fingers drumming about an hour ahead of time each and every time. I put on my denim wrap-around skirt and a bright blue tee shirt with a yellow fish in the middle, thinking it might give Layla and Bobby Ray's girls a smile. It came with a matching headband, so I wore that, too. I crept out, got all freshened up in the bathroom, and then looked for Momma and the Cadillac basket. Daddy sang as I rounded the stairwell,

Good morning to you! Good morning to you!
We're all in our places with bright, shiny faces.
Yes, this is the way to start the new day!

My friends and me sang this song every single morning at Miz Katie Claire's kindergarten five years ago. Lisbeth sang it before me, Meri before her, and Will before Meri. Daddy just never stopped singing it after all those kindergarten years.

"Morning, Daddy! Where's Momma?" I asked.

"She's waiting for you in the VW. It's about 150 degrees in that car, so you'd best use your running feet."

"Well, she said eight o'clock."

Daddy smirked. "I know, I know. But you know good as me that meant seven o'clock. Plus, she needs to get back in time to take all you kids to the pool for the afternoon." Even though we had a right nice pool that I could see from where I stood, when Ida Bell wasn't here, Momma preferred that we were out of the house if she and Daddy were working at their offices.

"Did Momma talk to you this morning, or is she still all quiet?" I asked.

"She's raring to go. It'll do her good to get things settled with Layla and Bobby Ray. Be nice for her to see Mr. Twilly, too."

"She must have the basket. It was sitting on the table when I went to bed last night."

"She sure does, and you outdid yourself, Gracie. I especially like those orange and blue Auburn ribbons."

When an Alabama baby was born, it automatically belonged to two things: a church for being raised up proper, and either Auburn or Alabama football. My grandmother was a dorm mother on the Auburn campus. Both my parents went to school there, and I guess all us kids will, too. When Momma and me visited that dirt-floor trailer, I noticed just one thing taped up on the wall: a front-page newspaper article with the headlines, "Punt Bama Punt."

Now, I was only two-and-a-half years old when the "Punt Bama Punt" game was played, but I remember it like it was Christmas day. The Alabama football team sported themselves a 10-0 winning season, and was supposed to beat Auburn with their eyes closed, then claim the national title. For the first three and a half quarters, that's exactly what happened. In the very last ten minutes of the game, though, Alabama punted twice to Auburn, and twice Auburn blocked the punt and ran the ball right straight into the end zone for a 16-16 tie. Auburn kicked the extra point for a 17-16 Auburn victory! I knew those little girls back at the trailer would like to have some navy blue and burnt orange ribbons.

I gave Daddy a hug. He held the door open for me and quoted,

The world breaks everyone, and afterward
Then my turn,
some are strong at the broken places

The morning air was thick with honeysuckle scent, and I stopped just a minute to take it in and give Daddy's quote some thought. I wondered if he had Layla and Bobby Ray in mind as being broken, or if he thought these words because of Momma. The VW sputtered, so I called out, "I'm coming, Momma!" before she left without me.

"We are going to Layla and Bobby Ray's, right, Momma?"

I asked, surprised by Momma's blue jeans and tee shirt, and her missing wine-colored lipstick and blush. Come to think of it, I'd never in my life seen my Momma in a pair of blue jeans.

"Why, certainly, Peamite. What ever do you mean?"

"You don't much look like yourself, is all."

"I just didn't have the energy this morning, Gracie," Momma said, and we were off. "Why don't you find us some news on the radio?" In other words, Momma didn't feel chit-chatty.

"Yes, ma'am." I twisted the knob on the Sapphire II AM radio. Static. Pushing one of the station-finding buttons landed me on a news program, which I immediately tuned out, preoccupied still by Momma's looks. Her eyes seemed swelly, her face too white, and she was all hunched up over the steering wheel like somebody driving through a thunderstorm. The air around her was like the air around a storm: choky and hard to see through. She hardly moved, and didn't utter a single word the whole way out to Layla and Bobby Ray's. When we pulled into their place, all she said was, "Remember your manners, now, Gracie."

"I will, Momma."

I lifted our Cadillac basket up over my head so the chickens couldn't mess with it. Momma knocked on the doorframe. "Layla, Bobby Ray? It's Sadie and Grace."

Layla came so fast it made me think she was just standing there waiting for us on the other side of that once pretty rose-bud sheet. "Hey, Miz Callaway," was all she could manage before letting her head fall into her hands, giving in to cries that were tied down before. Momma steadied her, strong and unbroken like the rhythm of a river. Momma didn't say a word. She just let Layla get it out. I circled my arms around both their waists and Layla's hurt swelled up in my heart and down my cheeks. My crying took Layla by surprise. She stroked my hair, and seemed to lose some of her own sorrow by reaching out to me. "Aw, now, don't you cry, too, little girl. It ain't nothing to do with you."

The girls came busting through, and ran right past their momma like they were getting used to seeing her with her heart poured out all over the place. I sure enough understood that. "Look at all them bow ribbons!" the older girl said. "What you got all them for?"

"For you and you sister. Wanna look at them?"

Her eyes filled up with starlight, and I knew deep down that that little girl and her sister would be the two reasons and the two reasons only that Layla and Bobby Ray would pull through their angel baby dying. The three of us went through the whole Cadillac basket while Momma got things squared away with Layla and Bobby Ray about the baby's funeral arrangements. They decided not to have a viewing on account Layla and Bobby Ray said it would be unbearable. Momma didn't give a clear answer when Layla asked who'd bought the country wooden casket, so I knew right off it was her. She said it was painted baby pink, and had a padded pillow and soft muslin on the inside. Momma told Layla and Bobby Ray not to worry if the casket looked too little, because babies are laid in there in a curled up position for good resting. The three adults agreed that the little angel baby would be buried day after tomorrow.

I liked those little girls with their red-dirt feet. They seemed to like me, too. As Momma and me backed out of the driveway, they peeked out from the rosebud sheet, one on each side. I hollered out to them, "Next time, why don't y'all come out to my place? We can play with the dogs and eat lunch up in the tree house." Next thing I knew, they were running for the Volkswagen, all squeals and giggles.

"Girls, now, how many times am I gone have to tell you not to run out here in this chicken mess without shoes on them feet of yours?" Layla said. "Get on back in this here house and show the Callaways you got some idea of what manners are. Grace didn't mean for you to come running home with her just now. I'm so sorry, Miz Callaway; don't pay them any mind," Layla said, shuffling the girls back behind the sheet.

"Oh, now, Layla, they're sweet as sugar. We'll come by soon so they can come over and play. We'd love to have them," Momma said as we turned toward home.

Momma's charm and strength must've got trapped in that dirt-floor trailer. Soon as it was out of sight, she disappeared, too. I could see her all right, but she was gone, she was gone, she was gone. Just a blank person, with empty eyes and a poured out heart. I kept quiet, and it surprised me when we turned into Mr. Twilly's place. "Just go tell him hey real quick, Peamite. I promised him we'd come by."

I didn't ask Momma why she wasn't coming along, too

scared of the answer. Mr. Twilly was a man to count on. There he was, dressed for Easter Sunday on a Friday, big old grin clear across his face. "Miss Grace, you done gone and made my day! Want to swing over to Conecuh County with me?"

"I sure do," I said, and climbed into the biggest basket I could find, one made for hauling cotton or corn.

"That one there can hold clear up to 125 pounds. You and your momma both could swing!" Mr. Twilly said, eyeing the VW. Mr. Twilly wasn't one to meddle, but I could read the concern for Momma written in his gentle eyes. "All abooooooooard," he yelled to the heavens. "This here's the Twilly Express. Next stop, the great Conecuh County of Alabama! You ready Miss Grace?"

"Yes, sir!" Mr. Twilly carried me in the basket over to the sycamore tree just off the porch that marked the county line. On one side was Monroe County; on the other was Conecuh. He swung me to the right and yelled, "Monroe!" To the left and yelled, "Conecuh!" I chimed in as he swung, both of us chanting, "Monroe! Conecuh! Monroe! Conecuh!" Mr. Twilly's white teeth glowing behind his smile, the warm air breezing through me, and the joy in his voice helped me let go of my disappearing momma for a few wondrous seconds. "Monroe! Conecuh! Monroe! Conecuh!"

"Hold on, passengers! We about to bring this here Twilly Express to a stop. Please come ride with us again!" Mr. Twilly put me down, but neither of us could stop laughing. He reached into his suit pocket and pulled out the tiniest basket I'd ever seen, no bigger than a minute. I didn't even know how a person's hands could make something so small. "This here's for your momma. Tell her it's sure enough small, but holds a whole heap of love," Mr. Twilly said.

I smiled. "I surely will! See you real soon!" I said and hugged his neck. I just knew that Mr. Twilly's itty-bitty basket would make Momma's mood blossom. I ran to her quick as my legs would carry me. Soon as I handed it to her and told her what Mr. Twilly said about it holding love, she went and welled up with tears, gave a long gaze and a wave to Mr. Twilly, then headed us toward home without looking back.

❦ 18 ❦

"GRACIE, can you say this: 'The skunk sat on the stump. The skunk thunk the stump stunk, and the stump thunk the skunk stunk?'" Daddy asked, knowing I was quiet because Ida Bell wasn't here. Daddy could make a stop sign laugh if he aimed to. I was in no mood for tongue twisters, though, or for going to the Capote Park pool with Will, Meri, and Lisbeth like Momma wanted. "Can I come to work with you, Daddy?" He and Momma both had to go back after lunchtime.

"Well, sure you can sometime. You wouldn't enjoy it this afternoon, though. I've got one meeting after another with fall semester closing in." I didn't care whether or not I'd *like* being at work with Daddy, I just wanted to be there instead of where I was going.

"Okay, kids, go get in the car. I canNOT be late for work!" Momma called. "Do y'all have sunscreen? Water? Snacks packed? Change of clothes? My phone number? Daddy's, too?" Momma was running around gathering candy wrappers and tissues that had landed in the trashcans in the ten minutes since Daddy emptied them last. This was garbage day, and she couldn't stand for there to be even one scrap in a trash can. "I just wish for once all the cans in this house could stay empty for five minutes!" she said. Then she headed to the fridge and started pouring half-empty orange juice gallons into Tupperware pitchers so she could get the gallon jugs out with today's trash.

Momma's office was just a few blocks down the road from Capote Park, so she was the one who dropped us off. "Now, I don't want you talking to anyone, you hear me, *anyone* you don't know. And stay away from that snack bar. It's too removed, and there could be meanness going on out there. You know there's nothing going on there that *should* be going on. Oh, and no jumping off that high-dive, I don't care how many times you've done it. Have you seen the bloodstains where a little boy jumped off and hit his head on that diving board? Of course, then he nearly drowned before the lifeguards even knew about it. They're all too busy flirting with each other to do their jobs."

Us kids glazed over as Momma ranted on and on. We could have given her the same speech, we'd heard it so many times. "Do y'all *hear* me?" she asked.

"Yes, ma'am," we all sang at once, swallowing our giggles.

At Capote Park, we set up our towels in a row and laid out in the sun. Will wouldn't let me lay by him because if I had my eyes shut, I needed to be touching someone so I'd know they were there. Truth is, any time Ida Bell was away from me, I shook a little on the insides till she got back. "I don't want a long white spot on my tan where your finger's been! Go lay by Meri or Lisbeth," Will said. Either they didn't care, or they were just being nice, but my sisters never once said anything about a streaked tan on account of me. While we laid there hearing the sounds of summertime, I got to thinking on what Blake and Rebel had said about Bible verses at Whet Whetstone's place. It occurred to me that there could be a verse I needed, a verse to help out with Momma's sadness.

When we all cooled off in the pool, it was Will's shining moment. He took turns throwing us girls up in the air so high we backflipped before hitting the water. Other kids lined up to be next. There was one trick reserved just for us Callaway kids, though. Will went underwater and came up with Meri on his shoulders. Then they both went underwater and came up with Lisbeth on Meri's shoulders. Then they all three went under and came up with me on Lisbeth's shoulders. There we were, all four stacked one on top of the other. I had the view of the whole pool, and even the snack bar. The lifeguard's whistle sounded right off. "No!" was all she said with a pointed finger. We dismantled.

But Will never could resist a little trouble. Said if we'd all do it one more time, he'd buy us each a Snickers from the snack bar. When the four of us popped out of the water a second time on each others' shoulders, the lifeguard didn't sound her whistle; instead, she came down from her stand, walked importantly over to us, and gave us exactly five minutes to vacate the pool area.

Great. It was only one o'clock, and Momma wasn't coming back until she got off work around five-thirty. How were we going to spend four and a half hours in this Alabama heat without a pool to cool off in? "I'm going to the snack bar, and nobody's telling Momma or Daddy," Will said.

"Wait a minute, Will. There's something we should all talk over while we got a minute," I said.

"What?" Will asked, with those eyes that said *What could you possibly say that would be important to me?*

"Well, everybody knows Momma's been wanting to move away from Daisy Street. Have y'all heard her talking about moving out of Monroeville, though?" Checking each other's faces, they all shook their heads, no.

"I heard her and Daddy talking about it yesterday," I said. "She wants to go to a bigger town. She was right serious, too. Her voice had a get-it-done tone about it."

"We can't move now," Will said with his face all scrunched up, like I was stupid for even thinking Momma was for-real. "Not just any old school has a junior high marching band. Plus, Momma and Daddy *think* the band keeps me out of trouble. If we ever do move, which I doubt, it'll at least be a few years off."

"I don't know, Will," Meri said. "Momma's gotten so miserable lately that I think Daddy'd do anything to get her to feeling better." Meri's words carried more wisdom than mine did for Will. She was his little sister, but I was his littlest sister.

"I know. I've just steered clear of Momma lately. Even when I'm not in trouble, I feel like I've done wrong around her," he said.

"Hey, y'all, I've got an idea," I said. "Over at Whet Whetstone's burned up house, folks have been getting Bible verses to help out with problems. We could walk over there, get us a verse so we'd know how to solve this moving problem, and be back before Momma's supposed to pick us up." Every last one of them looked at me like I'd sprouted antlers on top of my head.

"What in tarnation are you talking about now, little Grace?" Will asked.

"I'm not kidding, y'all. Remember the police saying Mr. Whetstone was hunched up over something when they found his burned up body?" I looked at Lisbeth for some sign that she knew what I was talking about.

She said, "I remember *that*, but what's it got to do with getting Bible verses?"

"'Cause Mr. Whetstone was covering up his Bible, and apparently it wasn't just any old Bible. If you go over there, the Bible is near the front door, and if you stand before it, the pages flip until they land on a verse meant for you to read." They all still looked at me like they couldn't believe their sister would buy such nonsense.

"Okay, y'all, listen here. Rebel Wadsworth and Blake Cooley both went over and got verses. Rebel's was about getting right with God, and Blake's talked about why he's so poor. Now, are you going to tell me that those strange things don't mean something more than coincidence?"

"You know, Grace, sometimes I forget you was dropped on your head as a baby," Will said. "I'm out. You girls go on and prance yourselves over to a burned up house for no good reason. I'm having a candy bar in the shade. I owe you three a bar, too, so if anybody wants to come with me, now's your chance."

I hated being treated like a baby. "I really don't care what you think, Will," I said. "I'm going to Whet Whetstone's with or without you."

"She can't go by herself," Lisbeth said to Meri.

"All right. The girls will go. I don't want to get in trouble for going to the snack bar anyway," Meri said. "With Momma's mood lately, if we got caught at the snack bar, we'd be on restriction till Christmas. We can get to Mr. Whetstone's and back in plenty of time for Momma not to know a thing." So the three of us headed back to Daisy Street, thanking the good Lord that it wasn't far out there under the midsummer sun.

❦　❦

Once we reached the place where Mr. Whetstone's house used to be, I pointed up the walkway. I could tell Meri and Lisbeth were just trying not to embarrass me by going along with this, so I wanted to make it quick. We neared the charred space where the foyer used to be, and the once quiet wind kicked in something mighty. Trees wrestled with each other, and scorched grass flew up in our faces. Our hair was blowing every which way, and we couldn't even hear each other talk. Meri and Lisbeth both had question marks in their eyes, like maybe there was something to my story after all.

Ashes swirled up from the rubble, pinching our eyes, but
we moved on closer. I motioned to Mr. Whetstone's old Bible,
laying open just past the foyer, and Meri and Lisbeth traded
doubtful glances. The Bible was covered in ashes that were
disappearing in the wind. Lisbeth took the first step, and Meri
and me followed close. As we stood huddled together, the old
book flipped from back to front and back again. Somewhere
in the latter pages, it fell strangely open and still while the
wind stayed all wild. The three of us sisters crouched down to
read the small print, and here's what we found:

...Old things are passed away; behold,
all things are become new

Still unable to talk above the noisy wind, we turned toward Daisy Street. About halfway there, Lisbeth let out a
gasp that even I could hear over the swirly winds. She stopped
dead and hunched over. "What is it, Lisbeth?" I yelled over the
commotion.

Unable to catch her breath, Lisbeth pointed both hands at
her left foot. A nail stuck straight out the top. It had punched
clear through her flipflop and pointed into the heavens from
between two of her pretty painted toes. Lisbeth's eyes were
part wild, part pain, and part uh-oh because she knew this
meant Momma'd find out we were here. Meri and me helped
her sit down, while blood collected around the nail.

"I'm calling Daddy on the phone," Meri yelled, and ran
towards our house.

The wind took off with her, and soon as we could hear each other, I asked, "How bad is it, Lisbeth?"

Finally able to catch her breath, she said, "Real bad. Kind of like a bee sting, only throbby plus stingy. Why don't you pull that nail out for me, Grace?"

My world was already spinning and a cool sweat surfacing before she said that. When the air around me went dark, I lowered my head and closed my eyes so I wouldn't faint. "I will if you want me to, but I think we should wait on Daddy. I might make it worse." Hoping she'd think on something else, I said, "What do you think, *Old things are passed away; behold, all things are become new* is supposed to mean?"

"Maybe that we *are* moving, like the 'new' part means our new hometown." Dust collected in my very soul, rust up underneath my heart. Momma'd said she wanted to move, and now this verse said something to the same effect.

Daddy drove up, and he and Meri hurried toward us. He scooped Lisbeth up in his arms and we all headed for the hospital. Lisbeth didn't need stitches or a shot, but the doctor said to keep an eye out for infection that sometimes happens deep inside the bones. On our drive home, we stopped by the park to get Will, and we told Daddy about our famous Callaway shoulder stand getting us kicked out of the pool. Daddy wasn't so much mad as he was worried about having to let Momma know. My insides dried up on account of Daddy. He hardly spoke on the drive home, and my Daddy hardly ever never spoke. When we got inside, he called Momma to let her know we were all home already, and that she needn't stop by the pool. Of course, this raised her eyebrows, but Daddy real smoothlike just said he'd had a few extra minutes so he went on and picked us up.

By the time Momma got home from work, us kids had all grown halos and wings of gold. Supper was on the table. We'd all pitched in for Hot Potato Dogs, and the house smelled like a tailgate party. We sat politely, waiting for Momma to eat. Momma knew right off something was up. "Somebody tell me what's going on this *instant*," she said. Momma hated, and I hardly ever used the word "hated," to feel left out in the dark.

"It's nothing, Momma," Will said. "It's just tiring being out in that sun for hours. We're plumb wore out." The rest of us nodded in agreement, even my poor old Daddy. Daddy'd talked about lies of omission versus lies of commission before from the pulpit. Now, my Daddy was anything but a liar. Just this once, I believe he was forgiven for his lie of omission. He was just looking out for Momma so she wouldn't have to deal with the trouble us kids caused today.

Me? I never could keep anything from Momma, and doggonit if she didn't know it. After supper, she quizzed me till I was pinned to the wall. Our secrets came out the way throw up does: undigested, heaving, and smelly. I blurted out how we got kicked out of the pool and headed over to Whet Whetstone's where Lisbeth stepped on that dadburn nail. I told her Will was at the snack bar, too. We all four got put on restriction for a week. No friends, no going out, no nothing. Will, Meri, and Lisbeth gave me the silent treatment all night long. To make matters worse, while Lisbeth and me spent our silent night together in our room, we overheard Momma breaking down on account of what I'd told her.

"William, where did I go wrong? My children are turning into failures. Have I not tried hard enough with them? I have done everything known for a mother to do. What are we going to do with them?" Momma said to Daddy through shoulder-shaking sobs.

"Now, Sadie, none of that's true and you know it," he said. "Our children are the brightest kids around, and you're the best mother any kid could hope for. Things just seem worse than they are because of your work stress."

At that, Momma launched into a long, spiraly speech about everything that's ever even seemed slightly wrong. None of her children were polite. We never tried hard enough to keep out of trouble. The house was never clean, unless she saw to it that it was done. She couldn't stomach her job anymore. She'd never be able to find another job, though. Daddy's work took up too much time. We didn't have enough money to go on all the vacations we needed, or enough for Momma to have more jewelry. On and on and on it dragged. Daddy tried to comfort Momma when she let him get a word in, but eventually seemed to realize that Momma was stuck in her misery, and maybe didn't want help getting unstuck. I wondered what I might do, and deep down felt that disappearing was the only thing I could do to help.

I'd never in my life seen or heard Momma act like this. She was so polished in public, so bubbly and put together. She used to be like that at home, too. Lisbeth sat on her bed turned toward the wall as far away from me as she could get while having to stay in the same room. I wanted to ask her if her foot hurt, if she had any more thoughts about *all things becoming new*, if she pretty-please wouldn't be mad at me just this once. I knew better.

Our lamps were both out when Daddy tiptoed in. Embarrassed to see him, I played possum. Daddy rearranged my covers and kissed my forehead, then whispered poetry in my ear,

My sun sets to rise again

I breathed in his words with my next breath, and let them lullaby me to sleep, hoping the world would be sunnier come morning.

❧ 19 ❧

"LISBETH, Grace? Hop on up and get your room cleaned," Momma called from the hallway. "Meri, you, too."

"Just one Saturday, just *one*, I'd like to sleep later than the chickens," Lisbeth said to me. Tears of relief almost got away from me. I couldn't handle another day of her silent treatment, not on top of Momma's darkness and missing Ida Bell. Us Callaways could get right put off with each other, but once over, that was that. Lisbeth looked out our window, her blonde hair a mess but pretty anyway. Both my sisters were prettier than me. Folks think sisters don't think about such things; truth is, we think on them more than anybody. Lisbeth's eyes had a little slant that made her face her very own. Meri looked like Daddy. I favored Momma. We all three looked like sisters, though.

Each and every Saturday we cleaned the house all day, and I mean *all* day. Momma would come around in a little while for room inspection. It never once passed on the first try. "I'm not having this mess," Momma would say, snake-voiced, opening drawers and leaving them open. That meant they needed redoing. Problem was, the drawer was nice and neat before she slung it open. "Good Lord, just look at this closet. And what in the world is that under your bed? Haven't I taught you better than this?" she'd say. We could've played a recording and saved her some time.

"Lisbeth, what exactly does Momma mean when our drawers aren't straight enough?" I asked.

"She don't mean a blessed thing. Just making her point, is all."

"Well, what is her point?"

"That she's in charge, and can keep us in our room as long as she pleases."

I guess Momma didn't want to be bothered by the goings-on of four kids over the weekend. I also guessed that having a clean house meant more to her than spending time with us, seeing as how the weekend was really and truly our only chance to be together. I was glad to be sharing a room with Lisbeth instead of shuffling things from one spot to another all by myself. Lisbeth and me made up games to clean our already-clean room. We tossed a pillow up in the air and "cleaned" whatever it landed on. Or, we ran around the room, counted to ten, then stopped and "cleaned" whatever was close by. Today, though, we had lots to talk about: Lisbeth's foot, getting in trouble, and *Old things are passed away; behold, all things are become new.*

"Did you tell anybody about that verse?" Lisbeth asked.

"Not a soul. You?"

"Well, I guess not, since I've been stuck in here. What I can't get over isn't the verse, but the whippy winds over there. Maybe we *should* move away from Daisy Street."

"Away from Daisy Street, or to a whole new town are two different things."

"Agreed."

The doorknob turned and we silenced on cue. Momma's face said the words before her mouth. It was wound up tight, all her features scrunched up toward the middle. "I don't understand why you girls don't keep your room better. I did not raise you in a barn, and I certainly did not raise you to embarrass your entire family in public," she said. *Please, please let this be a quick one,* I thought. These tirades of Momma's wore me clean out. Even though all I did was stand there and take it, once Momma finished getting on me I always felt exhausted like I had run full speed all the way over to Ida Bell's house. Too bad I couldn't do that right now.

Lisbeth tuned Momma out. She pretended to organize the bookcase, her back turned. Momma left every drawer open. The streetlights were on by the time Momma pronounced our room "Good enough, I guess, since it's so late and we still have tomorrow to think about."

The rest of the night was spent getting presentable for Sunday church: nails clipped, hair trimmed, washed, detangled, and rolled up with bobby pins that had to be slept on all night long, dresses and button-down shirts ironed, shoes polished bright white since it was after Easter and before

Labor Day, and, since it was summer, laying out white gloves with matching hats for us girls. Sure would be nice to spend Saturday watching cartoons and riding bikes on Daisy Street like Harper and Blake Cooley. Lisbeth and me dropped into bed, tired from boredom and tired of each other.

Sunday morning was a fresh start. Momma wouldn't be grumpy on account we'd pretty much be in public. Church basically stretched out all day long. Daddy preached part-time at the Excel United Methodist Church, a little country flock where everybody knew everybody and all their business. After the morning service, we were always invited to someone's home for Sunday lunch. Today, we went over to the Watson's. They were real nice folks, and let us play with their rabbits out back while lunch warmed in the oven. Once seated at the table, Momma politely said, "Now, Lou Ellen, you've *got* to tell me your recipe for this tasty stew."

"Oh, it's real easy, Sadie. You mix water, garlic, onion, bay leaves, little dab of sugar, pinch of salt, Worcestershire sauce, and paprika with your browned meat. Simmer that for a couple hours, then add your carrots and cook a little longer. If you like your gravy thick, dribble some cornstarch in there. Now, be sure to cook that rabbit meat to high heavens; it's wild you know."

Will, Meri, Lisbeth and me froze, wondering what in the world to do with the half-chewed rabbit in our mouths. Good gosh, we were just outside playing with those little bunnies! If we spit it out, we'd get skinned alive back home. If we swallowed and then threw up at the dinner table, well, that would be worse. Will snuck his chewed stew into his napkin, and then excused himself to the restroom. Momma glared us girls down, one by one, over her glasses when the Watsons weren't looking. Without making a single sound, she clearly said, "I don't care what it takes. Swallow."

Sunday night was good to get to. Ida Bell would be back come morning-time. Lisbeth and me were already under our covers when Momma's down-in-the-dumps voice came through the wall. "I get to Saturday, and can feel myself un-knotting. My fingers unclench and my shoulders rest where they're supposed to. But by Sunday, I'm already knotting up again," she said to Daddy. For her, weekdays were spent in the thick of work stress, and weekends were spent worrying about the weekdays that were always on their way back around.

20

COME Monday morning, Ida Bell's face was a cool afternoon swim. "Ida Bell!" I said, and hugged me a tight one. "What are we gonna do today?" I asked, taking in her rosy scent.

"Gracie-girl, me and you gone look after this here dog that done showed up on your front porch. See here?" she said, pointing out of the glass front door. That there was the sorriest looking mutt I'd ever seen. He was huddled up in a ball, his ribs sticking out every which way. He was no color at all, and yet every imaginable color. Brown here and black there, gray patches, dirty white, and then there were the places with no hair, what I guessed people called "the mange."

Now, I was a sucker for a stray dog. I knew, what with already having fourteen dogs, that there was no way in heaven we could keep this one. "What are we gonna do with him, Ida Bell?"

"Well, now, we gone clean him up and carry him over to my place. My children'll look after him."

Going to Ida Bell's was sweeter than chocolate pie at Sunday night Fellowship Supper. There was a tire swing, a treehouse, and a garden the size of my whole backyard. Then I remembered. "But, Ida Bell. I'm on restriction for getting kicked out of the pool at Capote Park. Didn't Momma tell you?"

"Mmm-hmm, she sure enough did, Gracie. Do I look like your momma? Come on. We got lots to do before this mutt sets foot in my car," she said, sticking out her I for our handshake.

We set the stray down in a metal washtub out front. He smelled like the back end of a billy goat. On their way out the door for work, Momma and Daddy both asked Ida Bell what she planned to do with him, but Ida Bell just kept scrubbing and humming "Precious Lord," not once looking up. Every time I got in trouble for something, it took Ida Bell nearly an entire week before she'd speak to my parents again.

Ida Bell named the stray Billy, I reckon on account of his smell. Once we let him out of that washtub, he took off like he'd stole some food, running around the yard and trying his best to rub dirt back into his bald spots. I guess dirt felt better than nothing at all. We fed and watered him, and then Ida Bell put him in the kennel cage she always kept in the back seat floorboard of her car in case she found an animal needing help. It was the first time in my ten years of knowing Ida Bell that I actually got mad at her. "Why in the world does Billy have to get in that cage?" I asked. I was sure the dog'd be just fine up in the seat like everybody else.

"Well now, Gracie-girl, it's for his own good. A scared animal gone feel safer in a snug place. Plus, we don't want him jumping back and forth between the seats and hurting himself, now, do we?"

"No, ma'am," I said, and felt like a mess for doubting her.

Once Billy was all settled in, we headed out. It only took about ten minutes to get to Ida Bell's from our house. I always appreciated that. Thought if I was ever in a pinch and needed to get to her, I could make it that far on foot if I had to. We got on Route 21, rode south past the Monroe County Hospital, past the college where Daddy worked, past the Monroe County Airport, and then it was all cotton and corn till Frisco City.

After a few turns on red dirt, Ida Bell's place turned my head like a garden resort people buy tickets to get into. Pink, deep purple, white, and red crepe myrtle trees lined the sidewalk leading up to her front porch, and summertime flowers framed her little white house. The heavy, sweet magnolia blossom scent met me even before I got my car door open.

Ida Bell's place was just exactly right. The snug, one-story house had a wrap-around porch where cushioned rocking chairs called me to stop a while and listen to bird whistles. When we got inside, Ida Bell let me do whatever I pleased. I ran around the house, seeing that everything was the same: deep freezer full of vegetables for winter, pretty patchwork curtains hanging from windows, leftover cheesy biscuits on the stove, free for the taking.

"Now, Gracie-girl, I'm gone let this here dog out and see

can he get used to things. You go on out back and get your lunch," Ida Bell said.

"Yes, ma'am. Can I bring you something?"

"Mmm-hmm. I got a taste for some greens. Take this basket here."

This had to be one of my all-time favorite things to do. I got to pick my lunch right straight from Ida Bell's garden, so big I actually got lost in there a time or two. I kept my eye on the huge old sugarcane pot near the house to see my way out. Ida Bell and her family used to boil cane juice to make syrup, but now the pot was used as a watering trough for Apple Jack, Ida Bell's horse. Whatever I brought to the kitchen in my basket, Ida Bell and me would cook right then and there for lunch.

The summer heat lifted garden scents up to my face, freshness all around. The birds loved it here. They sang like it was revival time. I got a good share of purple hull peas. We both loved those. Then an ear of sweet corn for each of us, two of the reddest tomatoes I do believe I'd ever seen, a bushel of collards, and a mess of strawberries for dessert. I eyed the old cane pot and made my way back to the house.

"I'm ready, Ida Bell," I shouted, the cornbread scent stopping me. Ida Bell knew me well. There was nothing finer than cornbread to go with purple hulls.

"Let's us get these peas shelled over on the porch, Gracie." We propped ourselves in the rocking chairs and shelled till our thumbs turned purple. Then we shucked the corn, and took out the stems from the collard leaves. While our lunch cooked, we messed around with Billy to get him feeling at home. He and Apple Jack seemed to hit it off, at least until he jumped into her cane pot for a cooling-off swim. That horse whinnied right in Billy's face, and he swam around in crazy circles, howling like she'd bit his tail. We helped him out, then had a lunch as good as any holiday dinner.

"All right, Gracie-girl, we best be heading on back up Route 21 before your folks get off work. I don't suppose they'd take too kindly at my bringing you out here, beings you're on restriction and all." We did our handshake, a silent agreement never to tell.

"Ida Bell, may I ask you something?"

"Sure enough. What's on your mind?"

"You know how Momma's been crying a lot because of work?"

"Mmm-hmm, I sure do."

"I've been wondering if those other things are because of work, too."

"Now, what you mean by 'other things,' Gracie?"

"You know, like having to have all the trash cans empty at the same time. Or us always having to look perfect to go somewhere. Or having at least three locks on every door. Stuff like that."

"Mmm-hmm, I see what you're asking. She gots an illness, Gracie-girl. Ain't nothing she can do about it except move on through it. Now, I can't say it's all because of work, but I can say that work sure enough sets it rolling."

"If she quit that sorry job, would she get better?"

"In all honesty, I reckon not, honey-child."

"Why not, Ida Bell?"

"Your Momma's gone need some help before things get better. She gone need more than a new job." The flowers on the crepe myrtles that weren't open yet made me think. They were a lot like Momma. She had all this blossom inside that just couldn't seem to get out to the light. Maybe *Old things are passed away; behold, all things are become new* was talking more about Momma and less about moving. Maybe Momma could become new.

It sure seemed to me, though, that Momma wasn't ever gonna get out to the light all on her own. My Momma needed help. Right then and there my own light shone on some new thoughts. I knew, I mean deep down *knew* that the Bible verses over at Whet's carried for-real meaning. That knowing gave me a plan for helping Momma. I'd go back over to Whet's tonight after dark so I wouldn't get caught, and see what verse the Good Book opened up to. I'd use the verse to help Momma out tomorrow because if she would ever need it, it would be tomorrow. Momma'd come home after work and land right in her crying chair because she has to visit a home in the morning and take a little boy and girl away to live with a foster family. She knew them kids'd be better off in a new home, but she said pulling a crying child from its mother's arms leaves an image on a person for life. Ida Bell dropped me back off at home, and I made plans to get me that verse.

❦ 21 ❦

"H ARPER?" I whispered into the phone. If I got caught talking on the phone while on restriction, I'd get skinned alive.

"Grace, hey! Where've you been?"

"Restriction. We all got in trouble at the pool on Friday, and have been in our rooms practically ever since, except for yesterday when we ate *rabbit* over at somebody's house, and today when I got to go over to Ida Bell's. I can't talk long, but I sure need your help."

"Ooooh, secret help. This is fun! What is it?"

"Have you heard all the commotion about Whet Whetstone's place being preachy-haunted?"

"Well, yeah, but there's nothing to that. Rebel started it, and you know he lies."

"Like a no-legged dog, I know; but let me tell you, Harper, this time it's true. Can you meet me at the creek when the streetlights come on? I need a verse from Whet's place, and it's a long story, but I know for sure my sisters aren't going there with me. Don't wear flipflops!"

"Okay, Gracie, but all this is gonna do is prove I'm right about Rebel being a liar. I'll be there though."

At dusk I told Lisbeth my plan, and she agreed to cover for me if Momma or Daddy came looking. I crept through the house and out the front door so I wouldn't get the dogs roused up out back. I could already see Harper down by the creek, so I took off running.

"Hey!" I said, catching my breath.

"Hey! Do you still want to do this?"

"I can't exactly say I *want* to, but I've got to. My momma's in some kind of shape, Harper. She's been crying day and night, and talking about moving to a new town. If this even has a chance of helping her, it's worth it."

"Somebody's coming down the road, Grace! Duck down in the creek."

Harper and me crouched down into the brambles beside the creek. Problem was, though, Harper wore a pink dress that was trimmed in lace at the neck, sleeves, waist, and hem. This particular creekside grew pricklyash, and stuck out strong prickles from every which way. "Grace, this stuff's gonna rip my dress to shreds. My momma'll tan my hide!"

Blake came along just in time to hear. "Oh, right. Like you've ever had a spanking in your life. You girls digging up fishing worms down there?"

"Blake Cooley, you ought to know better than to sneak up

on people!" I said. "But since you're here, you and your filthy grocery store feet can come, too."

"I can come? Whoo-hoo!"

"Shhh! You are going to get me in more trouble than I can imagine! Are you a sandwich short of a picnic? You don't even know where we're going."

"You just never invited me nowhere, is all."

"Harper and me are headed over to Whet's for a verse, so we might as well all go."

"All right, then. But only if Rebel can come, too."

"Blake Cooley, I take back the picnic insult. That's the best idea ever to come from your brain."

Blake grinned so big I could see into tomorrow between his teeth.

"Rebel Wadsworth's got connections with the devil, I'm sure of it. Maybe it won't get so wild and spooky if he comes," I said. We headed toward Rebel's, each step churning up a bit of shiver that wasn't there before. With the houses spread far apart, and no lights burning at Whet's anymore, this end of Daisy Street was black as Momma's sadness.

In a million years, I wouldn't have guessed I'd be standing here knocking on Rebel Wadsworth's front door. His place was surprisingly lit up all over: every room on both floors inside, the front porch light, and even two spotlights shone on two huge planters on either side of the porch columns. Looked like a photo from Momma's *Southern Living* magazine.

Mr. Wadsworth opened the door. "Well, good evening

Grace and Harper and Blake," he said, his eyes squinted like a baseball was about to hit him between the eyes. I know good and well he was wondering what trouble Rebel had gotten himself into that we were fixing to tell about. "Come right on in. What can I do for you?"

"We were hoping to speak with Rebel," I said, my voice gathering quivers at thinking on what lay ahead.

"Grace, are you all right? You need me to call your folks for you?"

"Oh, no sir. I'm just fine. I'm a little out of breath because Blake, Harper and me were racing each other over here," I said, smiling pretty up at him and crossing my fingers that my face looked for-real. If Momma and Daddy found out I was messing around out here, I'd be grounded till I was twelve and Momma'd cry herself right to sleep tonight and the next night and the next.

"Is Rebel into something I need to know about?" Mr. Wadsworth asked.

"No sir, it's nothing like that. We just need his help is all," I said, nudging Blake so he'd speak up. Blake Cooley was the neighborhood liar, even though he didn't technically live in our neighborhood, and was always willing to share his talent if somebody needed a cover-up story in front of grown-ups.

"Yeah, I got my bike stuck over in the gully, and we could use Rebel's help getting it out," Blake lied, completely clear-faced.

Pleased at the thought of his son doing something nice

for a change, Mr. Wadsworth said, "Well, let me get him for you. I know he'd be happy to give you a hand."

Rebel appeared, but didn't speak to a single one of us as he closed his front door behind him. He perched his hands on his hips, cocked his head to one side, and raised his eyebrows, like, *Well, what?* "Rebel, you're coming with us. I'll explain while we walk," I told him.

Taken by surprise, Rebel followed me like I was his momma telling him what to do. It took some time before we could see our way again in the thick darkness after looking into the light at Rebel's place. The nighttime animals whistled their tunes, paying no mind at all to the fear sitting on my shoulders. The air still held the sweet scent of sun-warmed honeysuckle. The skies above hid their stars, their twinkles and hope just beyond eyesight. I wanted to stay right there at Rebel's while our way was still lit, but knew if I didn't get moving, I'd lose my nerve.

"I've got to get a verse from the Good Book at Whet Whetstone's place."

"What do you want me for?" he asked.

"Rebel, you're the meanest person I've ever known, so I figure you must know the devil himself. I want you to go over there and see to it that the devil steers clear."

Rebel raised an eyebrow in Harper's direction. "What's Harley going to do, smooth the lace on her dress and look pretty for the devil?"

"My name's not Harley. It's Harper, you no-name freak."

"Oh, excuse me. HarPER. That's *so* much better. Now you really sound sophisticated," Rebel said.

"I'll have you know I'm named after one of Monroe County's most prominent citizens, Harper Lee."

"Oh, he's so famous that I've actually never heard of him."

"Good grief, get an education, why don't you? *She* only wrote the Pulitzer Prize winning novel *To Kill a Mockingbird*. I guess you also didn't know that folks around here call her by her first name, Nelle, and I assume you also didn't know that "Nelle" is Miz Lee's grandmother's name spelled backward. Is there anything else you'd like to know?" Harper asked, her brow raised and hands on her hips.

Being stupid, even if you are a bully, was not highly favored in our community. Truth is, Rebel wasn't stupid. He just acted stupid. I wondered if it was like my Momma acting happy at work or church or the library even when I knew she'd love to sit down and have a good cry.

"Rebel, I was wrong to ask you to come," I said. "Come on Blake and Harper, I don't have time for his nonsense."

Blake spoke up. "Rebel here needs another shot, please, ladies. See, he's been working on having the fire of the Lord lit inside him." Blake fisted Rebel in the ribs with one hand, stuck his earlobe into his ear with the other. "Takes a person a bit of practice, is all."

Well, if that didn't beat all. Blake Cooley sounded rather polished. If I couldn't see him squishing his earlobe into his ear, and the crusty red leftover *something* from his supper splattered around his mouth, I might've thought he was someone else just then.

"All right, Rebel. Can you handle this, or not?" I asked.

"Yeah, but, did you hear what happened when Shelby Simmonds went messing around over there?" Rebel asked.

"I don't care, Rebel, I've got to do this! Are you trying to scare me?" I said.

"You need to know what you're getting into is all. Shelby Simmonds paid the Whetstone place a visit, and came out with a verse, all right. Only, it didn't come from the Bible book; it came from Wheaton Whetstone himself."

"You're not scaring me, Rebel. Now, come on."

"Let me finish, Grace." The very fact that he said my name made me stop and listen. Maybe that fire from his own verse was being lit after all. "Shelby never made it to the door. When she was a couple steps away, the wind picked up, she saw a chalky-looking man moving toward her, and he started yelling out a Bible verse, something about falling into hell, into a fire that never ever goes out. Shelby's skin got all hot the way a sunburn feels, and she ran out quick as she could."

"How come you think Shelby didn't just make all this up for a good story?" Blake Cooley asked.

"Cause all the hair on her arms was singed like she'd been near a sure-enough fire. Folks been calling her 'Peaches' now, cause she looks like she's got peach fuzz on her arms where there's supposed to be hair," Rebel said.

"Look, peach fuzz or not, chalky ghosts and all, I've got

a mind to do what I need to do. Are you coming with me, or not?" I asked, and searched the eyes of Rebel, Blake, and Harper.

Harper began walking toward Whet's. Blake Cooley stood there, his hands in his pockets, shuffling his feet side to side. It was Rebel who spoke up first. "All right, Miss Callaway, let's do it."

The only thing stranger than knocking on Rebel Wadsworth's door was standing between him and Blake Cooley, Harper on Blake's other side, all our arms locked together, walking like we were one person up to the old Whetstone front foyer. There were no words between us, just straight-forward determination.

Then it all began. From the sidewalk, we heard what pain sounds like. The wind whirled in circles, carrying aching moans in dizzying coils around our heads. Voices ranting on about fire and burning forever in hell screeched out at us like we were in a Halloween haunted house. I pushed us on. Keeping my arms locked with Rebel and Blake and Harper's, I steered us to Whet Whetstone's Bible and watched its pages somersault in the wind. Once it fell quiet, just enough moonlight highlighted Isaiah 58:10 for me to make it out:

If you extend your soul to the hungry
And satisfy the afflicted soul,
Then your light shall dawn in the darkness,
And your darkness shall be as the noonday

❧ 22 ❧

SAFE in my bed, Lisbeth close by, last night's fear wouldn't let me alone. After we got our verse, Harper, Rebel, Blake, and me shot off to each of our homes fast as our spaghetti legs could run. I slept a smidgen last night, but kept waking to nightmares of fists pounding on church pulpits and heaps still smoldering over at Whet's, images that set my thoughts on constant fire about extending my soul, satisfying the afflicted, and light dawning in the darkness.

I needed to call Ida Bell before she came over this morning. Momma told me never, ever to call Ida Bell because it's so much work for Miz Peggy Pearl to get her to the phone. Miz Peggy Pearl was in charge of the telephone party line, the phone line shared among her family and several other families nearby. This was always interesting because people could hear other people's conversations while trying to have their own. Since they shared the telephone that was at her place, Miz Peggy Pearl was always real gracious about running next door whenever we called for Ida Bell. If I could just talk with

Ida Bell real quick, I could ask her to bring her Bible commentary so I could figure out just exactly how I was supposed to "extend my soul to the hungry."

"Momma? Could you please, pretty please help me call Ida Bell real quick?" I asked as Momma considered her outfit in her full-length mirror.

"Grace, it's six o'clock in the morning. What are you doing out of bed?"

"I just need to talk to Ida Bell, Momma. I don't know how to do that party line telephone, though."

"Now, why in the world do you need to talk to Ida Bell this early? She'll be here shortly." Momma never liked for anything to be private between Ida Bell and me. For that matter, she didn't like anything private between Daddy and me, Lisbeth and me, Meri and me, or Harper and me, either. "Now, when you need something, you can talk to your momma, okay?"

"Nevermind, Momma. It can wait till Ida Bell gets here," I said, and pretended to go back to bed while Momma was still preoccupied with her looks. What I for-real did, though, was close mine and Lisbeth's bedroom door, and head on down the stairs and out the door. Ida Bell's place wasn't that far, and I could probably get there before she left to come here, especially if I cut through the woods and Blake Cooley's neighborhood.

I knew I'd better get up Daisy Street a little piece before heading into the trees, or else the dogs would tell my secret. Just past Whet's, I sloshed through the gully leading into the woods. This place sure enough was bigger now that I was out here all by my lonesome self. The morning songbirds took the edge off the shakiness creeping around my back. I sang along with them, deciding on Ida Bell's "Precious Lord" because when I sang it, I heard Ida Bell's voice harmonizing with mine.

It wasn't long before all I could see was woods in front of me and in back of me, and for some reason that spooked me up, down, and sideways. Remembering all the meanness Momma said was on Blake Cooley's side of the woods, I turned my scaredy-cat self right around and high-tailed it back through the trees, back to the gully, back down Daisy Street, and right back up the stairs to Momma's room. She was dressed now, and gathering things for her purse.

I caught my breath, and said, "Momma, that phone call to Ida Bell really can't wait. Will you do it for me? It's about a surprise for you," I lied, fingers crossed behind my back.

"All right, we can try. But I'm not going to let that phone ring too many times. I don't want to wake up Miz Peggy Pearl." Momma got out her little blue book where she kept people's addresses and phone numbers. It was also the book where she made her lists. When we shopped at the grocery store and something needed crossing off, she used Liquid Paper instead of just marking through it like most folks. I figured this was part of what Ida Bell called Momma's "illness." Momma dialed the number for Miz Peggy Pearl in the kitchen while I got on the dining room phone to listen in. It only rang twice before Miz Peggy Pearl picked up.

"Goooooooood morning!"

"Miz Peggy Pearl?" Momma shouted, like she was talking to someone in her nineties. "It's Sadie Callaway. How you doing today?" she said, trying to make her voice stand out over the other party-liners.

"Well, now, I'm just fine and dandy, how 'bout you? You and the children all right?"

"We certainly are. Grace is right here, and wondered if you might have time to get Ida Bell for her."

"Oh, now, I'd be real happy to run over. Let me hurry and see can I catch her before she leaves this morning."

"Well, I sure appreciate your trouble," Momma said.

"Okay, Momma, I can take it from here. Could you give me a minute with Ida Bell?" I asked. With a small huff, Momma disappeared. I knew, though, that she would keep herself close enough to hear at least my end of the conversation, so I picked my words just right.

Ida Bell came on the line. "Gracie-girl, everything all right, now?"

"Hey, Ida Bell! Yeah, I'm fine. Remember that surprise I was telling you about, the one for Momma?" Ida Bell was real good about playing along, especially if I mentioned Momma.

"Sure enough, go on."

"Well, we're gone need your Bible commentary book for it. Do you think you could bring it with you this morning?

"Mmm-hmm, sure thing. And I also got some collard greens I'm bringing over."

"You got *what?*" I asked, not able to hear real well over

some lady who was gossiping about another lady being too showy at a wedding reception.

"Some greens, Grace. I'll be there directly," she said, and I heard a quick click. I could still hear the gossip going, and wanted to listen in, but Momma appeared somehow just at the right time to tell me to hang up.

Ida Bell got here about the time Momma and Daddy left for work. Her bag was extra bulgy, but she didn't take out the commentary book until they were good and gone.

"Now, Gracie, what you need this for?" she asked, pulling out the huge book.

"Ida Bell, me and Harper and Blake Cooley and Rebel Wadsworth went next door to the burned up house and got me a Bible verse so I could help Momma, and it looks like a real good one, if I only knew what it meant."

"Now, slow down a minute here, Grace. You done been over to the Whetstone place?" Ida Bell asked. I had tried to breeze over that part. There may have been only one thing Ida Bell and Momma agreed on when it came to me: I was not supposed to be over at the Whetstone place.

"I had to, Ida Bell. You said Momma needed help, so I aim to help her. I couldn't think of anything else to do but get a hand from Wheaton Whetstone himself, who I believe is in heaven and in good standing with angels and such. And, Ida Bell? Something real's going on over there. There ain't no way around it."

"What you mean, honey-child?"

"It was more than just a verse, Ida Bell. It was like heaven opened up to give me the verse, but hell was opened, too, to scare me away. The winds and skies and trees were demons with their arms reaching for me, and just listen to the verse where Whet's Bible opened:

If you extend your soul to the hungry
And satisfy the afflicted soul,
Then your light shall dawn in the darkness,
And your darkness shall be as the noonday.

"Well, I'll be a monkey's uncle. That's a good one, all right. But we don't need no commentary, Gracie. This here's real easy."

"What's it mean to *extend your soul to the hungry and satisfy the afflicted soul*? Momma don't need food; she needs, well, what *does* she need, Ida Bell?"

"Now, I'm guessing your momma might be hungry for knowing she belongs somewhere, you know, like she's *really* wanted and welcome."

"But Momma's always wanted, and nothing but welcome."

"Course she is, Gracie-girl. It's just that everybody knows that but her. When folks take on melancholy, things get twisted and stretched, all confused-like. Now, you can't very well convince a person with an illness that they belong, but you can sure enough let her know that no illness gone stand in your way of being her daughter."

"Oh. Thing is, it is in the way. I don't feel nothing *but* in the way when Momma's crying. Makes me want to disappear, hoping that'd be one less person for her to worry over. Maybe if I try to get her mind off being sad, she'll smile a little more."

"Well, now, Gracie-girl, all that's up to you. Don't take on the world, you hear? A ten-year-old ain't half of a twenty-year-old! Grown-ups got grown-up-and-still-growing problems. Sometimes it's hard to break through. You know what, though? Your momma's gone know you care. Simple as that sounds, that can do a whole heap of good for a person."

❧ 23 ❧

I KNEW Momma'd come home from work a mess. I didn't even know she was in the house before her pretty hymn-playing ambled through the walls. She must've come through the formal front entrance, which we never used, to avoid seeing anybody. That hurt my feelings just a tad. Momma wanted me to come to her when I had bruisy feelings, but she sure didn't do the same.

By the time I reached the stairs, Momma was about to play my favorite part of "It is Well with My Soul," the swelling resolve of the first verse,

Whatever my lot, Thou has taught me to say
It is well, it is well with my soul

Remembering the last lousy time I interrupted Momma's *It is Well with My Soul*-playing, I decided to keep her company in a different way. If I danced to her beautiful music, she'd have to keep the song going. I needed to be careful not to look over at Momma and embarrass her.

Her playing filled me up and got my body moving. As she crescendoed into *Whatever my lot, Thou has taught me to say,* I glided into the living room to express the triumph and strength of the *It is well, it is well with my soul* part that was coming. I imagined myself moving in an elegant and quiet ballet sweep like I'd seen on TV.

Instead of letting the glory fulfill its purpose, Momma sank into the piano, sending an ugly mash of notes into the air. This was no mistake, for my momma never once made a mistake playing hymns. Not once. Layered on top of the hurt of knowing Momma'd snuck in the house to avoid me, now sat guilt. Guilt of not letting a person alone. Why didn't I just sit and listen to Momma's song? Somewhere deep inside, though, I knew good and well Momma didn't want to be let alone. Trouble was, she didn't know how to be with me and her pain all rolled into one.

"Grace, please go get me an ice pack for my throbbing head," she whispered, unable to manage anything more.

Extend your soul. This was my chance to help Momma, and by God, I was going to sit and talk with her if it was the last thing I ever did on this earth. I ran into the kitchen where, nowadays, she always kept an ice pack in the freezer. "Here you go, Momma. Is it real bad?" This was hard. It would've been a whole lot easier to just go hide than be here with Momma's misery hanging in the air. Momma didn't answer me. She nodded her head "yes" in a painful, slow way that told me not to ask any more questions.

I did anyway. "Momma, did you see the Old Yella hibiscus shrub all full of blooms when you came in? The purple and pink ones are blooming, too. Want me to go pick you a bundle?

"No, Peamite," she whispered, her eyes closed. "I just need to sit here. Go on and feed the dogs, why don't you?"

"Yes, ma'am." Now, feeding fourteen dogs took a chunk of time. I had to gather up all the pails scattered from here to kingdom come. The puppies, their little black noses and floppy ears everywhere, ran around with their bowls in their mouths, but they sure enough didn't bring them back to the porch. The leftover food had to be cleaned out. The water bowls had to be emptied and cleaned, then filled again. And while doing all this, the dogs jumped all over me. It was a real feat. Whenever Momma said, "Go feed the dogs," what she meant was, "Go away for a solid stretch of time."

Thirty minutes later, my go-away chore was done. I figured that was enough time for Momma to sit still, and thought maybe she was ready for some pretty hibiscus flowers by now. I picked her the biggest, brightest bouquet of my life, fifty flowers, I'd guess, and arranged them in an old pickle jar because it was the only thing big enough to hold all that beauty. The sunny yellow petals of each flower overlapped with each other. Momma and me were like that. Sometimes I didn't know where she ended and I began, or if that line between two people was really and truly there. I found Momma in her rocking chair. "Momma, I've got a surprise for you. Close your eyes!"

I walked over to Momma, and sure enough, her eyes were hidden under the ice pack. "Okay, Momma, you can look now."

"Grace, please. Not now," she said, still talking low like her head would explode if her voice raised up to normal.

"They're hibiscus blooms, Momma. And I put a little wild rose here and there, too. Your favorite, remember?"

Momma stopped talking altogether. Stopped listening, too, I guessed. I set the flowers on top of her sewing basket beside her chair, and kept thinking on what to do. More than anything, I wanted to talk to Ida Bell. She always knew what to do.

I didn't want to let Momma slide down into her own world for the rest of the night. If I didn't get her talking again, and quick, that's exactly what would happen. This moment, this instant, mattered. Panic began in my heart and struck lightning-like through my arms and legs, sending me into a tremble like before I ran to get the dogs during Whet's fire. Once Momma was gone, she was gone until morning. Gone, gone, gone.

Ice cream! Momma loved nothing more than a bowl of soft-serve chocolate ice cream on a hot day. Come to think, Momma loved ice cream any day, even in December. "Momma, when your head's better, let's me and you walk on over to the drugstore and share an ice cream."

"Now, Grace, I've told you my head hurts," she scolded, her voice raised up to normal for the first time since getting home.

"But, Momma, they've got chocolate in their soft-serve machine today. We'll ask Miz Calhoun to sprinkle chopped almonds on top the way you like it."

"Grace Callaway, go to your room right this instant! I don't want to hear another word," she snapped, and then sank. The raising of her voice gave her head a pounding she didn't need. I was paralyzed, thick, like I was trying to walk through waist-deep mud. That mud darn near swallowed me up. How could I extend my soul to a momma who was locked up tighter than the town bank?

24

I CAN count on exactly two fingers the number of times my momma's snapped at me before today. The first time happened in the car with Meri and Lisbeth. Momma and Daddy had run in the post office, and told us to stay buckled in. Just as Momma and Daddy slipped out of sight, Meri started jumping this way and that, trying to open the door, her eyes all wild-like. I kept locking the door on account we were told to stay put.

Thank the good Lord Momma and Daddy got back quick, because Daddy realized right off that Meri was choking. I swear, my daddy stuck his hand straight down her throat and pulled out an entire yellow-green June apple.

When Momma found out what I'd done, she said, red-faced and dark eyed, "Grace, why in the name of heaven didn't you *help* your sister? You're old enough to tell when there's an emergency going on. I expect better from you." Ida Bell said Momma just felt guilty for leaving us in the car.

The second and last time until today Momma snapped at me happened when I thought I was turning on a light switch at the Auburn University dormitory. See, my grandmother was a dorm mother there, so we got to visit all the time. Problem was, when I flipped that switch, an alarm sounded and lights flashed every which-a-way. I pushed the switch back down quick as sand, but nothing stopped. All of a sudden, college kids ran down the hallways and in every direction. Couples from the lobby stopped their smooching and shot out, too. When the fire department arrived with their sirens on and the firefighters unrolled their hoses, I just about died. I'm sure that a little piece of Momma did die.

Of course, anything embarrassing to my momma in public was ten times worse than something happening at home with the curtains drawn. "Oh, Grace, I just cannot believe you went and did this," she said, her voice low and hurt, which was way worse than just getting a good yelling. "You have embarrassed our entire family. I just don't know when we'll ever be able to go back to the campus."

After today's ice cream idea went south, I went to my room like I was told, but didn't want my crying heard. I smushed my face down into my pillow where I made a real big mess. I wished I never had to come out of my room again. I hung my pillowcase up to dry on the hook behind the door, and heard Daddy come home. Then, I heard him and Momma talking across the hallway, a conversation that turned my blood to blue ice.

"Sadie, what's going on?" he asked, knowing it was something more than the usual.

"William, I am a complete and utter failure. Grace, our

little angel girl, was trying to help, and I let her have it. I don't know where she's gone off to now. Probably out in the woods, down at the berry patch, or maybe even to Ida Bell's. I really hurt her," she said.

"She'll be all right, Sadie. Grace knows you didn't mean it. She's a right smart young lady. I'll find her. I have some news for you that I think will help."

"Now, William, I am in no mood for news or help. Just see me to the bed." I never understood why Momma's bad mood gave her the right to tell Daddy what to do.

"Hear me out for a minute, Sadie," he said. "I've been offered a job with the state. If we decide I should take it, you could quit your job. Tomorrow. You could look for something else, something with less stress involved. Now, isn't that music to your ears?"

"William, I'll never find another job around here. You know that."

"That's part of the good news, Sadie. It's not around here. The job's in Montgomery, 82 miles up the road. There are bound to be more jobs there for you. And the schools are solid."

"But it's going to be Will's first year with the marching band and all. He will have an absolute conniption. You know the biggest problem though: Gracie. How would we ever tell her we're leaving Ida Bell?"

Cold seeped through my wet face and out of my palms. My heart thumped loud enough for me to actually hear it, and it was fast like I'd been running a race. A race it sounded like I just might lose. Leaving Ida Bell? How could Momma even say words like that? I reached for my picture of Ida Bell up under my pillow and stared into her gentle, smiling eyes, always, always, always looking at me, looking out for me. A fine layer of dust snowed down and settled over my soul.

25

NEXT morning I didn't venture downstairs till I knew Ida Bell was there. I didn't want to talk to another soul. On my way to greet her in the garage, I caught sight of a message on the kitchen chalkboard:

FAMILY MEETING
7:00 TONIGHT
NO EXCUSES!

Up rose the sludge through my brain that had crept in last night listening to Momma and Daddy. In my entire life, not one single family meeting had ever been about something good. I got to Ida Bell quick as I could, jumped into her car before she got out, and buried my head in her lap. "Well, now, good morning to you, Gracie-girl!" she said, putting the car in park.

"Morning, Ida Bell. There's a message up on the chalkboard saying we have one of them family meetings tonight."

"Mmm-hmm. Your brother in trouble again?" she asked while we headed inside.

"Well, probably, but there are two things I thought might be on Daddy's mind. One, I really made Momma sink low last night. You know how when one of us kids gets into trouble, Momma and Daddy like to make an example out of it for the other three? I think the meeting's gonna be along those lines."

"Mmm-hmm," Ida Bell said, shaking her head that she understood and pulling out the grater for the cheesy grits she was fixing to make. She never asked me questions about trouble I got in, but she'd always listen if I told her.

"Or, the second thing might be this crazy thing Momma and Daddy were talking about last night. Daddy told Momma he got an offer to work in Montgomery. They were talking all serious-like, but they wouldn't ever *really* move, would they, Ida Bell?"

"Why you think that, now?"

"Because you're here and not there."

"Well, now, Gracie-girl, your folks gots lots to think about 'sides where I am. They gots to worry about the family as a whole, mostly about your momma. When the momma in a family ain't flourishing, don't nothing go quite right."

"Ida Bell, you're my family as much or more than anybody calling themselves a Callaway. So if it's family we're talking about, well, it's obvious that the Callaways won't be setting off to Montgomery."

"Oh, Gracie, you sure enough right. Let's us not fret over this just now. That talking between your folks might've just been your daddy's way of pulling your momma up from her misery. Tonight's family meeting probably gone be just like all the rest. Your daddy'll have him a list to talk from that your momma done put together. It's gone say:

1. Dirty clothes go in the hamper, and nowhere else.

2. No boys allowed in the girls' bedrooms, and no girls allowed in Will's room. Isn't proper. Girlfriends and boyfriends can visit in the formal living room, with our approval, of course.

When she said this one, Ida Bell raised her eyebrows and pretended to look over her glasses, just exactly like Daddy would do. We both doubled over. I couldn't help but laugh, but the truth is that there's nothing I hate more than a family meeting. Momma'll be sullen, won't say not a word. She'll sit in that chair and act like us kids have ruined her life. Daddy'll say, "Your poor mother works herself to the bone, and you kids just aren't grateful." Family meetings were less about what was on the list and more about Momma needing to hear Daddy get on us. She always said she had to be the villain because Daddy wouldn't discipline us enough. Truth was, Daddy expected goodness while Momma required one hundred percent perfection.

Ida Bell and me ate our cheesy grits, and then she decided to get our minds off that dadburn meeting. "Gracie-girl, let's us head up Daisy Street and on over to the drugstore. Ain't nothing finer than a grape soda with peanuts to put the mind at ease."

"Sounds good! And I have to show you the hibiscus blooms on the way."

"Well, now, I done saw that big old bouquet yonder on your momma's sewing basket. You pick all them?"

"Yep, I sure did. You want 'em?"

"Well, now, ain't those your momma's?"

"They *were* Momma's, but I want to give them to you like I should've in the first place."

"Why you want to go and give them to me, child?"

"It's a long story, Ida Bell."

"I ain't in no particular hurry, Gracie-girl."

"You've smiled at every single flower I've brought you since I was little."

Tears spilled out of nowhere right along with the whole story about how I'd talked to Momma when all I wanted to do was run, how I'd gotten her flowers and tried to get her to come out for ice cream with me; and, how not a bit of it did a lick of good.

"Now, what's all this fuss?" Ida Bell asked, wiping my face clean. Ida Bell never let my tears fall far.

"That stupid Bible verse I worked so hard to get from Wheaton Whetstone did about as much good as a tore up dollar bill."

"Now, why you gone go and say a thing like that?"

"I tried my hardest to extend my soul to Momma, but I sure as heck didn't see no light dawning in the darkness like the words promised."

"Oh, now, I bet it ain't as bad as you thinking. Who

wouldn't feel loved with a great big bundle of flowers like you done picked?"

"Momma yelled at me, Ida Bell. And that was after she told me to go feed the dogs."

"Your little ol' momma raised her voice to you?"

"Yes, ma'am. She surely did."

"Mmm-hmm, well, ain't that something. I don't reckon I've ever heard her voice much louder than a little chickadee."

"Well, this was more like a squawking yellowhammer."

"Your Momma loves you, Gracie-girl, more than the Alabama heat is hot. When you was born into this here Callaway family, it was like a little bit of starlight was sprinkled into folks' eyes. You don't remember, but your momma lost her daddy not too long before you was born. And the circumstances was tough, too: car accident, and the folks from the other car dropping a lawsuit on your momma's momma for nary a good reason. Your grandmother got even meaner than before, and she never was no picnic for your momma in the first place.

But then you came along, this pretty little baby, could fit in a shoebox. You wasn't no more than five pounds when they brought you home from the Monroe County Hospital down the road. Life started all over again for your momma. Which means it started all over again for the whole Callaway bunch! Now, you bear with that momma of yours. She gone come around yet."

❧ 26 ❧

AFTER all the crying, wishing, hoping, and failing of yesterday and this morning, I was plumb wore-out. Felt like work just to blink my eyes. "How 'bout that grape soda now, Ida Bell?" I asked.

"Oh, that do sound mighty fine, Gracie," Ida Bell said.

Ida Bell and me bought the same thing each and every time we walked down to CK's Drugstore. "Gracie, how 'bout you go get the peanuts while I get the grape soda, you hear?"

"Okay, Ida Bell. I'll meet you at the soda fountain in just a minute." When I caught up with Ida Bell, Miz Calhoun was firing her usual question after question. With a little listening, I realized they were about my momma.

"Now, Ida Bell, I haven't seen Sadie Callaway in just ages. Is there something going on I should put on my prayer list?" Miz Calhoun asked.

"No, now, Miz Callaway just as fine as a blue morning! How 'bout you?"

"Oh, you know me. I never miss a beat. Now, is Sadie out of town?" she pressed on.

"Well, no. She's right busy what with her job and four children to look after."

"Hmm. She will be coming to the children's benefit supper this weekend, right?"

"Now, I couldn't possibly know all the goings and comings of a busy lady like Sadie Callaway. I'll tell her you was asking about her, though. You have a real nice day, Miz Calhoun," Ida Bell said, and motioned me to come on outside.

"Whoo-ooo, if that lady don't beat all I ever saw, Gracie! Now, she ain't got no business meddling around in your momma's affairs."

"I know, Ida Bell. I'm gone tell Momma when she gets home tonight."

"Well, now, I suppose we could just keep it between us, Gracie-girl."

We got comfortable in the rocking chairs on the drugstore porch, and plunked our peanuts into our grape sodas. Then came my favorite part. We sipped our drinks without one care in this world, and pretended we owned all of CK's Drugstore. We greeted the people who came like we appreciated their business. "Now, you just let us know can we help you find something," Ida Bell offered with a wink in my direction.

I didn't want to think on going back home where that family meeting was drumming its fingers on the table. Deep inside, I knew good and well it wouldn't be about the dirty clothes hamper. Wouldn't be along the lines of girlfriends and boyfriends, either. If I could just sit right here on this porch with Ida Bell forever, I'd surely-may-do do it.

27

AFTER Ida Bell left our house, Daddy started setting the supper table, pulling together fixings for Hot Potato Dogs and summer squash. Momma had disappeared into her bedroom, and it occurred to me that a long time had passed since I'd seen her last. I went into the kitchen to help Daddy. "Gracie, come here. Hurry!"

"What is it, Daddy?"

"Let me tighten your nose. It's about to fall right off and into the hot dogs!" he said, serious as a diamondback rattlesnake and pretending to screw my nose back into place just in time.

By the time all us kids placed our napkins in our laps, Momma came out from her hiding spot. Right off, the air grew smothery and hovered in our faces. The pressure was on to follow each and every rule of etiquette. Again. And once again, I excused myself, choosing a growling belly over possibly being snapped at by Momma for exactly the fourth time in my life.

"Excuse me, please," I said, and placed my napkin just so.

"You feeling all right, Grace?" Daddy asked.

"Yes, sir. Ida Bell and me had a late snack is all."

"All right then. Seven o'clock in the den, okay?"

"Yes, sir." The same "Please, excuse me" from Lisbeth, Meri, and Will followed and we all disappeared into our bedrooms. If nobody was around, maybe that family meeting would be called off.

"What do you think Daddy's got to say, Lisbeth?" I asked.

"Oh, you know, same like always. It'll be about keeping the house clean, behaving at church, talking nice to Momma. I don't know why we have to do this *again*," she said, throwing herself onto her bed, letting the pillows cover up her head. I was fixing to mention Daddy's telling Momma about the Montgomery job offer when Daddy called out, "Giiiiiiirls! Will! Y'all come on to the den, now." Lisbeth let out a moan like she was being thrown into a briar patch.

First thing I noticed downstairs was that Daddy wasn't holding his usual list. Momma sat there, not looking at any of us. She was supervising Daddy, and I figured that was the only reason she wasn't back in her bedroom. Will, Meri, Lisbeth, and I were waiting for Daddy to let us have it, when Daddy said, "Kids, there's something we need to tell you." Momma gave no sign that she was part of that *we*. Nothing. She stared out the window beyond the trees, beyond Monroeville, beyond us all.

"A real good opportunity has come along for us. The executive director of the Commission on Higher Education called and offered me a state job working out of Montgomery. The office is on Court Square, where all kinds of Alabama history has happened. This morning, I called back and took the job. I need to be there well before the academic year starts up again in the fall, and we need to get y'all settled in before school. Fact is, we'll be packing up the moving van this Friday."

"Friday, as in two-days-from-now Friday?" Will asked, panic taking over his eyes.

"Right. It's fast, I know; but, we just can't pass this up," Daddy said.

Will huffed so loud he scared the dogs out on the porch, then shoved a copy of *To Kill a Mockingbird* off the end table as he exited, saying nothing to my daddy. Momma found this worthy of breaking her silent trance. Through clenched teeth she said, "Will Callaway, that is a *signed* copy of my favorite book, and Miz Nelle never signs copies. Pick. It. Up." Will turned back and picked it up, but then tossed it onto the table with a sneer aimed straight from his eyes to Momma's. For once, Daddy let it go, watching Will disappear downstairs.

"What about my friends and school?" Meri asked, her hands opened, waiting to clench the answers.

"And all the dogs?" Lisbeth said, affirming with Meri that moving wouldn't work.

"Is Ida Bell coming?" I asked. Daddy rubbed his forehead like it hurt bad, and I had my answer. Meri had hers, too, but Daddy at least said the dogs were coming.

"Now, girls, this move is going to be hard on all of us. It's gonna be the hardest on your poor momma, though, so I want you to think on that instead of yourselves. Your momma'll be searching for a new job, new church, new friends, new everything. She'll be getting you into new schools. This'll turn out for the good; it's just going to take some time and everyone's cooperation," Daddy said with raised eyebrows, and squinted eyes that said, *I expect you to rise to this occasion.*

Out came the preacher in my daddy. Out came a blue glare from Meri, clench-toothed growls from Lisbeth, and tears from someplace deeper than my eyes that were crying them.

"Girls, you've gone and made your sister cry. I expected better. Head on up to your rooms and get to bed. We have a lot on our plate in the next few days."

The last thing I needed was my sisters getting mad at me again. Daddy walked over to me, and put both my hands in his. He whispered,

I thank whatever gods may be
but, I couldn't finish with,
For my unconquerable soul
Instead, I quipped with exactly the quote that came to mind,
Because I could not stop for death
and Daddy, through fisted feelings trudged out the rest because he'd never leave me hanging,
He kindly stopped for me
His eyes filled with heart, Daddy said, "Sweet Gracie,"

Tis not too late to seek a newer world

I countered, my eyes directly on his,

I exist as I am, that is enough

Then Daddy,

To not dare is to lose oneself

Me again,

Dismiss that which insults your soul, . . .
whatever satisfies the soul is truth

Daddy,

Let your soul stand cool and composed before a million
universes . . . in the confusion we stay with each other, happy
to be together, speaking without uttering a single word

With that, the ancient words fell back to the grave. We fell, too, into each other's arms. Daddy steadied my trembling shoulders. I let my head rest on him, the weight of my mind carried by another, and let my spirit muddle through an endless, black tunnel.

🌿 28 🌿

I MUST'VE fallen asleep in Daddy's arms, because I woke up tucked in my bed around midnight. My mind didn't give me one second's rest. Almost before my eyes were opened to the blackness and blueness all around, I landed right back inside the dark tunnel from before, remembering all too quickly that I hadn't dreamed up that family meeting. Lisbeth slept hard, tissues wadded up on her nightstand. I sat straight up, breathed in deep, and snuck out of the bedroom. If ever in my life I needed a Bible verse worth reading, it was this moment right here.

All was calm, the kind of calm that rises up goosebumps on your arms before a storm. I tiptoed downstairs, through the foyer, and out the front door. My eyes took a minute to adjust to the darker night outside, but I could make my way good enough without a flashlight. Little by little, I could see the driveway, then the oaks, then the leaves on the oaks. Lightning bugs blinked like twinkle lights, not brightening my way in the least, but putting me more at ease about traipsing around out here all by myself. I thought I'd better take the driveway and then the street over to Mr. Whetstone's instead of cutting through the woods on account of the dogs. Ruby-Dee would for sure let Momma know if she caught on that I was meddling around out here in the middle of the night.

The oaks stretched their arms out to me, familiar friends of old. An antique church bench sat up under the sixth oak on the right, and I swear Ida Bell was resting there, smiling sideways like she does when she's proud of me. Passing the last oak on the left, all the times Ida Bell had waited here with me for the school bus flashed as sweet memories before me. Each and every time, she squeezed me good and said, "I'll be right here when you gets back!" The water in the little creek rhythmed forward, Ida Bell's voice swooping over and through the river rock, calling out to me without words. She said, like always, she'd be here on my return.

At the road, my pace quickened to a jog, and then a sprint. Daisy Street was a stranger in the darkness, and I had to run straight through my fear to Mr. Whetstone's. My heart pounded double-time, and I knew better than to look back or even down. Fixing my sights straight ahead and running full speed was my only hope for not turning back. One thing my daddy taught me besides poetry, and taught me solid, was a proper fear of Hell. What in tarnation was I thinking heading right straight for it here on Earth?

I caught my breath at Whet's walkway, but couldn't rest long on account my legs would carry me back home without the consent of my heart. I'd never been exactly this alone in my life. It'd be all right if I never was this alone again. About halfway down Whet Whetstone's walkway, the warm air around me started a gentle twisting in a wide circle with me in the middle. Trees bowed to each other counter-clockwise all around, from my house up to Harper's and back again. Black and gray and white ash rose with the winds and chased after me, bees from a hive, stinging and all.

Frozen in fear, my eyes shut as tight as possible. My arms wrapped themselves around me, and I found my courage. I knew those arms were my own, but what I felt, and let myself feel, was Ida Bell's strong arms holding me tight, pressing me on. I set my sights on Whet's burned down foyer, then willed one wobbly leg in front of another until I got there. The winds picked up their whirls even faster, and the storm circle began closing in. Twigs snapped, and the woods between Whet's house and mine held a gray fog that turned to black in the deeps. I was smack-dab in the middle of a hellish tornado, a storm churned up by the devil himself to keep me from helping Momma, to keep me away from Ida Bell, to stop my getting whatever message the Good Book held for me.

Through it all, the crisp sound of fluttering, thin, sacred pages rose to me. Whet Whetstone's Bible, the one up under his very being when he died, lay at my feet. Whole chapters, books even, had ripped from its binding, and what was left was torn and weather-stained. Still, the pages flip-flopped in the winds. Golden flecks from the pages' edges sparkled. They settled at last, and I rubbed the ash and fear from my eyes to see what I had been given. A burgundy ribbon held the place, and even though the pages were only half there, there was no mistaking my verse. There was nothing else left that was readable except the swirly F beginning the next chapter. Mine said,

Find grace to help in time of need

Find grace to help in time of need, I whispered slow-like, soaking each word into my very skin and on through to my heart. I didn't need Ida Bell's thick commentary book to figure this one out. It was clear as smooth glass. An act of grace was somewhere close by, and was meant to help me in my time of need, maybe even help Momma in hers, maybe even keep me from moving 82 miles away from Ida Bell. Relief eased through me, and even though the winds still threatened and dust burned my eyes, I caught myself in a for-real smile. It seemed impossible to help my momma, impossible to have to move away from Ida Bell; but, looking for an act of grace felt all filled up with *possible*.

Jumping to my feet, I ran right straight back the way I'd come, each step a different word, "find . . . grace . . . to . . . help . . . in . . . time . . . of . . . need. Find . . . grace . . . to . . . help . . . in . . . time . . . of . . . need." Back down Daisy Street, back at my driveway where I felt Ida Bell waiting just like she said, over the creek, through the oaks, "find . . . grace . . . to . . . help . . . in . . . time . . . of . . . need." I slowed down on toward the porch steps, knowing I couldn't go inside breathing all loud and coughy. I could hardly wait to get to bed so I could wake up in the morning and find the grace that was rightfully mine.

29

"GRACIE-GIRL?"

"Ida Bell!" I said, and threw my covers aside. Lisbeth was already up and out the door, probably headed to visit with her friends while there was still time left. It surprised me that I didn't wake up earlier. I think the hope of my new verse gave my mind enough relief to let my body rest good. I got down the stairs quick as I could for my morning squeeze. Roses and sugarcane: I swear they ran right straight through Ida Bell's veins. I took in her scent and squished it deep down inside where it couldn't get out.

"Well, you sho 'nuff sunshiny, little lady. That family meeting must've gone right well."

"It was downright awful, Ida Bell, but last night I got the answer to my problem."

"Well, maybe you gone want to tell me your problem before you tell me the answer to it. Am I right?" Ida Bell asked. She could be right smart-alecky sometimes.

"Okay. At the meeting last night, Daddy said we had a good opportunity for our family, that he was offered a job up

Montgomery-way, and that he already took it. Ida Bell, we're leaving *tomorrow*." I thought I'd see the whites of Ida Bell's eyes, but she wore her same old gentle smile and calm eyes.

"I know, sugar pie. Your daddy done followed me out to the car yesterday as I was leaving and told me all about it. You've been on my mind ever since. I've been planning our first get-together for when I come visit your fine new place," she said, taking my hand in hers. I knew good and well Ida Bell was acting strong on my account.

"That's just it, though, Ida Bell. We're not really moving. Daddy just *thinks* we are."

"Now, why you say that, Gracie?"

"Because I got me a new Bible verse, and finally, this one makes some sense."

"You done been back over to that burned up place?" she asked, her smile turning down.

"Ida Bell, I *had* to, and I'm glad I did, and you'll be glad, too, when you hear what happened."

"All right then, Gracie-girl. I'm listening."

"I ran over in the dark, and the weather got real, real creepy-strange. Now I know that old Satan was hoping to scare me away on account I was going to be given something from the Good Book. But, Ida Bell, you were with me, and I just kept on going in the middle of that howling weather. I made it to the charred-up foyer, and Whet Whetstone's old book flipped in all that wind right straight to my verse."

"Well, what it said?"

"It said, *find grace to help in time of need*, and that's something I know I can do, Ida Bell. I got up this morning with a mind to find the grace that's gone keep me here with you."

Ida Bell spit out some cane into the trash. "Now, honey-child, I sure do likes to think we could stay together. But what if the grace you gone find is meant to help you and me with the being apart part?"

"Oh, no, Ida Bell. I'm sure as sunrise on this. I just gotta keep my eyes wide open so I don't miss what I'm supposed to find. Want to help me?"

"Well, I reckon I do, Gracie-girl. I promised your momma we'd get your room packed up today. Let's keep your Bible verse in mind while we work. I gots us a little coffee in this here pot, and I picked up some Krispy Kremes this morning. Figured we could use ourselves a donut or two."

I followed Ida Bell up the stairs, her roses and sugarcane flowing right straight up my nose. It occurred to me that roses and sugarcane might be part of the grace I was looking for, so I took note of that. "Ida Bell, you got any of that rosy perfume with you?"

She chuckled. "Now, why would I bring that over to your place?"

"I don't rightly know. I thought it might have something to do with my verse. Got any more sugarcane?"

"Mmm-hmm, a few sticks like always in my pocket. You wanting one while we work?" she asked, handing me one. It's shade was just a tad lighter than Ida Bell.

"Maybe so. Well, maybe after coffee and Krispy Kremes."

With the cream she brought, I got my coffee to looking

exactly like Ida Bell's skin, and imagined what I'd look like if I was her color. We drank, ate, wiped our sticky fingers, and managed to pack about ten boxes. Amazing how fast a box fills right up. Ida Bell organized my Sunday clothes while I went through my chest of drawers. I kept getting caught up in looking at all my saved-up things. One card I found was from my fifth birthday. It said, "For My Dear Daughter" on the outside. On the inside in flowy handwriting, it said, "Gracie, you're my sweet baby, and I love you thick and wide and up and down and inside-out and upside-down! Love, Ida Bell."

"You remember this?" I asked, holding the card up for her to see.

"Well, I reckon I do! You and me will have to be pen pals once you move up that road, Gracie. I likes letter-writing." I wondered if this letter might have something to do with my act of grace. I laid it down by my sugarcane, just in case.

We had just about finished mine and Lisbeth's room, and Lord knows I was tuckered out. "Ida Bell, do we have to do this all day long?" I was beginning to think my act of grace was somewhere besides my bedroom, maybe someplace with a fresh breeze and with the sun shining down on it.

"Oh, we 'bout done. Fact is, we gots to be done because I've worked up a little surprise for you. Why don't you put this here lacy pink outfit on and meet me in the kitchen in a minute or two."

"What is it, Ida Bell?"

"Well, I 'spect you'll see soon enough. I'll be on in the kitchen directly."

🌿 30 🌿

"Ida Bell, can I come down yet? I've got on that pretty pink dress," I hollered down the staircase.

"Mmm-hmm, come on, honey-child."

Dress or no dress, I steadied myself with the banister and skipped every other step on the way to Ida Bell. "What's my surprise?"

"Now, ain't you a sight? Pretty as an azalea bundle! Gracie, we gone have us a luncheon with a few friends out by the pool. Thought it might be nice to see some folks before…" Ida Bell stopped right there in the middle. She stared into my eyes, and I could see hers clouding over about to spill. "…before you gots to go. Come here to me, child." She held her arms out and pulled me in close. I guess we'd both been trying hard not to cry, which wasn't much like Ida Bell. Ida Bell always said our faces shouldn't get all tightened up when we need to cry. Said tears needed to be let loose like a stream, needed to be allowed to go where they was meant to. She patted my back and wiped us both off with her handkerchief. "All right, then. We best get on to our luncheon pretties."

Ida Bell covered my eyes as she opened the back door. "All right, now, sneak a peek."

I opened my eyes to a little piece of heaven right here in my backyard. The long wooden table where all us kids had carved our names was covered in a breezy lavender box-pleat tablecloth. That table was older than God, but Momma always said the older it gets, the better it looks. She should've seen it now! The lavender tablecloth was layered with a lacy white tablecloth on top. The benches on either side were covered in lavender linens, too, and the chairs at the table heads were draped the same, only with perfectly tied big bows in the back, a shade deeper than the chair fabric. Eight places were perfectly set. Each held a bright white dinner plate with a lavender napkin underneath cascading down the table's edge. On top of the plates sat small potted deep purple hydrangeas. The pots were painted light purple, and a dark purple ribbon tied around the edge said who sat where.

Pure delight filled me clean up, and I thought Ida Bell's eyes might just spill again. I took in more of the fancy table. Each place had a Mason jar filled with summertime peaches and blueberries, and in the middle of the table there was a white cake trimmed in purple hydrangeas. There was all kinds of party food on each side of the cake: cucumber and cream cheese tea sandwiches, gourmet crackers with Vidalia onion dipping sauce, cinnamon pecans, hushpuppies, good Lord, I don't know what all!

"Who'd you invite, Ida Bell?" I asked, looking at the plant ribbons.

"Well, Harper, of course. Blake Cooley and Mr. Wadsworth."

"Rebel Wadsworth?"

"Might surprise you how much you gone think about him once you're gone. I want you to know you did all you could to be friends with someone who sho 'nuff needed a friend! Oh, and your momma's gone bring over Layla and Bobby Ray's girls."

"Momma's coming?"

"She gone fetch them girls and drop 'em off on her lunch break. She won't have time to eat with us, though. Gots to be getting back to the office. I figured me and you could carry the girls back home, or maybe this here gentleman could."

I heard him before I saw him, a voice merry as a parade, "Anybody wants a ride to Conecuh County?"

"Mr. Twilly! Thanks for coming!" I said, and got me a hug.

"Well, now, I don't know if it was me Ida Bell wanted, or if she invited me for my world famous Twilly-made lemonade! I gots two pitcherfulls, one for your guests, and the other for us two. Ours could make the Mona Lisa squint, I 'spect!" He went right to the table and poured his Twilly-made lemonade into beautiful green glass tumblers at each place setting.

"Ida Bell, when'd you do all this?" I asked.

"Oh, now, Gracie you know I gots a little can-do magic in me when I needs it."

Harper, Blake Cooley, and Rebel Wadsworth all showed up together, all talking about how they couldn't believe I was moving. Ida Bell invited them to find their seats. I eyed the table again, along with my guests, looking for what might be the act of grace I was expecting. Then, the sound of Momma's Mercedes pulling in got my attention. "Excuse me, please. I need to run see about the last two guests," I said and headed toward Momma and the girls.

"I'm so delighted you could come over!" I said to them as they got out of the back seat, each one wearing the pretty pink hair bows I'd given them. They were all squeals and giggles, and I held both their hands and brought them over to the luncheon table and started giggling, too. Ida Bell had placed them on either side of me. I was seated in the middle of the table on the side facing the pool. Directly across from me was Harper, and Blake and Rebel were on either side of her. Ida Bell and Mr. Twilly sat in the captain's chairs at both ends. The dogs barked from their kennel run. Ida Bell got them all worked up because they knew anytime she put them in there that she's gone bring them her homemade party treats. She called them pupcakes instead of cupcakes, which I thought was right cute, and made them from flour, eggs, oats, and sugarcane juice.

"All right, now, folks, let's have ourselves a party. Just help yourself to what tickles you. And remember, at any party of mine, folks can have cake first, in the middle, last, or the whole time. Don't matter none to me!" Ida Bell said.

Blake Cooley looked around like he was guilty of something, then grinning ear to ear and showing the space between his teeth, he pulled out a bright orange Tupperware container from under his chair. He set it on the table, an awful clash with Ida Bell's china and purples, and announced, "This here,

Grace, is what I've been trying to get you to try over at my house since way back when. It's pickle toast. I could *never* let you leave off to Montgomery without a try."

This was what I'd managed to avoid *since way back when.* "Why, thank you, Blake. That was kind of you," I said, and opened the God-awful container. A swirl of flavor rose, first sautéed Vidalia onions, then toasted, buttered cheesy bread, and finally, dill pickles. It was like a souped-up grilled cheese, which happened to be one of my favorite foods in the world, 'sides blackberries. I didn't want anybody to see my fingers crossed for good luck, so I crossed my toes instead and tried Blake Cooley's pickle toast. I'm telling you, that dish, if placed on a nice serving platter, could become a dinner-on-the-ground favorite.

We passed Blake's Tupperware and the respectable serving plates cordially and said what we knew about Montgomery, Alabama. We came up with things to do on the Alabama River since Montgomery sits smack-dab on its bank.

"Grace, remember when my family and me went to Montgomery, and we boated to that restaurant upriver? It was a real pretty place with outdoor seating and fresh seafood," Harper said.

"Yeah, I do remember that. Seems like y'all had a lot of fun," I said, and Harper nodded.

"You could go deep sea fishing!" offered Blake.

"Blake Cooley, I'm moving *north*, not down to the gulf," I told him. If I couldn't see Blake Cooley right here in front of me, I'd swear that boy'd never traveled any farther than his front porch.

Layla and Bobby Ray's girls hadn't said boo, so I wanted to make them feel part of things by getting them in on some conversation. I realized I didn't even know their names, and thought how strange to feel like they were old friends of mine. I looked over at the older girl's hydrangea plant. The deep purple ribbon said, "Wynn," which I imagined to be her momma's maiden name. I snuck a peek at the little one's name, which was "Raychel," probably after her daddy, Bobby Ray. "Wynn, what do you think of Montgomery?" I asked.

Wynn lowered her chin and held her hands close to her heart. "Oh, I don't know nothing about it, but it sounds closer to Auburn. Maybe you'll get to go to a ballgame," she said, quiet and sweet like a little bunny rabbit talking.

"Oh, I'd sure like that. Maybe sometime you and Raychel could ride up and go to Auburn with me. I know my way around campus pretty well." Little Raychel giggled at the sound of her name being said.

Once we'd all had our fill of goodies, Ida Bell passed around pre-made cards to gather up my friends' addresses and phone numbers. She also gave them all cards to take home with my address.

"Why's this say 'Care of the Alabama Commission on Higher Education' instead of a normal address?" Rebel wanted to know.

I told him, "We're gonna be living on one of the state campuses in faculty housing until we find our own house. Once we do, I'll get you my new address."

Ida Bell'd also gotten clean white tee shirts for us all. All eight of us took turns pressing our hands in paint and then leaving our handprints on everybody's shirts. Raychel asked if she could do her feet, so we all had the cutest little footprints ever seen on our shirts, too. She chose blue paint, and when it mixed in with the orange dirt on her feet, it came out like an original piece of Auburn art. Then, we signed our names and hugged each other goodbye, pinky promising to write all the time. Ida Bell handed each guest their little potted hydrangea, and said to plant it someplace special, to remember.

"We'll let you know if we get any more good messages from Whet Whetstone's place," Rebel said, and Blake Cooley nodded along.

"And I'm gone have to ride up Montgomery-way soon and deliver you some Twilly-made lemonade! Maybe even bring your riding basket and see can we swing you into the next county from there," said Mr. Twilly, all his teeth showing from his grin.

"I'm sure gonna miss you, Gracie. We'll be best friends forever, no matter what," Harper said right into my eyes, into my heart.

The little girls kept quiet, but hugged me tight. Mr. Twilly showed them to his truck, where they giggled at getting to ride home in the back, which was all laced with snowy locks of leftover cotton. Once Mr. Twilly pulled out to the driveway, I ran behind them, and they whooped and hollered past all the oaks, darn near waving their skinny little arms off. Blake Cooley, Rebel Wadsworth, and Harper walked home from there. I watched each one, feeling in the breeze that my act of grace was somehow swept up in it and swirling right around me.

"Thanks, Ida Bell, for all this."

"Oh, you mighty welcome, Gracie-girl," she said. "Could you give me a hand in getting some of this stuff to the car?"

"Sure thing." Ida Bell boxed up her linens from the table and chairs.

"How 'bout carrying this over to the car? It fits right on the back seat," she said.

I took the box, breathing in the leftover smell of cake and good friends coming from its inside. Opening the back door of Ida Bell's long blue car, I stopped dead. I knew right off that there it was. The act of grace that I'd been looking for, so hoping for, was sitting right there in Ida Bell's back seat floorboard.

❦ 31 ❦

IDA BELL'S kennel cage! I set the linen box where Ida Bell told me, and stood there, thoughts swirling round and round like a cinnamon bun. This was just exactly what I'd been looking for! I glanced over at Whet Whetstone's, and whispered a quiet "thank you" for the wind to carry over there.

I wouldn't have ever believed that Ida Bell's kennel cage could be my salvation, my way out of leaving her. But gosh doggit, there it was. That dog kennel, the very one I got so worked up about because a stray was put in it, just might save my life. The more I thought about it, my plan of grace unfolded clear as angel wings. Tomorrow, I would squeeze myself into the cage and cover up with the blanket that was in there. Then, when Ida Bell drove home, I'd just ride on with her and live at her house. She'd be as thrilled as me. On moving day tomorrow, by the time everything was packed and my parents were ready to follow the moving van up the road, I would already be swaying in the tire swing at Ida Bell's house! This wouldn't exactly be easy to pull off, so I had to stop myself from biting my nails. If I didn't, Ida Bell would know right off that something had my mind.

I walked back over to help her finish cleaning up, but Ida Bell was already inside, singing "Precious Lord" while washing up the party dishes. That lady could work up a blue streak! Grabbing a drying towel, I said, "Ida Bell, you can stop helping me look for that act of grace. I already found it. I can't exactly tell you about it, but I know it was put there just for me. And Ida Bell? It was put there just for you, too."

Ida Bell stopped her washing and dried off her hands. Stopped her singing, too. She put both hands on my shoulders. "Gracie-girl, anything in this world put here for you was put here for me, too. And anything for me, for you. See now, we the same, me and you, just two waves in one ocean. I'm so happy you done found your act of grace, honey-child. Now, I gots to get on up the road to my house, 'cause I'm getting here early tomorrow to help out. Come here and hug me good." My cheek rested on hers, soft and warm, and in those arms, I breathed in deep, thinking on my life ahead as her little girl.

32

"**G**RAAACIE-GIRL. Wake on up, now, honey-child," Ida Bell said in a whisper-song voice. My hair was being stroked from my face, making way for the smoochie that followed. I didn't even have to open my eyes to name the gentleness, the rosy scent. "Good mooorning!" Ida Bell said.

"Good morning, Ida Bell. You smell all rosy-posy."

"Let me give you a little rosy-posy for yourself," she said, and rubbed my wrist with hers the way she knew I liked.

I put my wrist straight to my nose, and woke up some. Right off, I was in a real bad hurry to spring out of bed and down to Ida Bell's car to make sure the kennel cage was still there. I had to stay calm, though, or she'd catch on. I wasn't exactly trying to keep a secret from Ida Bell, but I didn't want her to get accused of helping me once my folks found out how I managed not to move 82 sorry miles up the road. I knew Ida Bell'd be happy to have me as her own, but I also knew she couldn't *take* me in order to have me.

Ida Bell's eyes were different, soft and looking right straight through me and on into the next day where she thought we wouldn't be together. "Gracie, why don't you get on out the bed and put these here berry-picking clothes on. I brought 'em from my grandbaby since yours are boxed up someplace," she said.

"We're going to the berry patch?"

"After breakfast, I gone carry you there," she said, her eyes with a little more happy in them than before. I smiled, but then a space welled up inside me, real quiet like a big empty church. I had found my act of grace, and now I had to carry it out. I reached up to Ida Bell and the shakes in my hands showed up.

She took my hands. "Gracie-girl, we gone be all right, now. All we gots to do is get through *Right Now*. All we gots to do after that is get through the next *Right Now*," she said.

Ida Bell didn't know my hands shook on account of my act of grace sitting in the floorboard of her long blue car. Bless her heart, she thought my nerves were shot because of moving to Montgomery, away from her. I'd never before kept a secret from Ida Bell except for surprises, and that was surely different.

"Gracie, we gone manage this day better if we gets moving. I'm gone finish up making a breakfast you won't believe, and when you gots your berrying clothes on, come on and join me."

"Be right down, Ida Bell." I put on the mismatched shirt and pants and took a look around mine and Lisbeth's room. She and Meri had stayed the night up the street at a friend's house, so it was mighty quiet up here. Even if I wasn't leaving Monroeville, I was leaving this house. There was the side window where I first spotted the fire at Whet Whetstone's. The place where my ribbon box sat. The bed that I'd been tucked into by Momma, Daddy, and Ida Bell, every night of my entire life. Out the front window the oaks stood at attention, their feet solid on the ground and their arms always held out to the sky. Past those, the road stretched to the berry patch. I figured Ida Bell and me could always walk this road and visit our patch, even if I didn't live here anymore. I breathed in a giant stream of air and walked down the stairs that had led me to Ida Bell morning after morning.

It was right busy around here. Boxes every which way, and Momma seemed to be in every room between mine and the kitchen. "Hey there, Peamite. You going to find Ida Bell?" she asked. Momma's hair was a mess, not the kind of mess like she'd had her head buried in her hands, but the kind meaning she was feeling carefree.

"Yes, ma'am. Momma, do you smell that?"

"Honey, all of Monroe County smells that. Run see what Ida Bell's cooked up for you." I swear my momma was smiling, and Lord knows it had been a good long while since I'd seen that.

"What is it, Peamite?" she asked, and I realized I was staring at her.

"Nothing, Momma. Just, you look right pretty is all."

"Oh, hush up now, and get on to your breakfast," she said with just the slightest twinkle.

"Momma, can I have some of your Chanel N°5?"

"Here you go. Now, run on." Momma rubbed her wrist on mine, and I took a whiff of what smelled like my very life: Momma's Chanel mixed in with Ida Bell's rosy scent, still on my wrist from earlier.

Ida Bell was waiting for me in the kitchen. "Mmm-mmm, Gracie, we gots us a mighty fine breakfast here! Come sit by me," she said. Ida Bell passed me a plate full of the best Southern big breakfast imaginable. There were buttermilk biscuits drowning in sawmill gravy, speckled cheesy grits, skillet fried potatoes, and my favorite fruit salad made with strawberries, grapes, and bananas.

"Well, I guess I'll never have to eat again, Ida Bell!"

"I 'spect not," she said, a giggle rising up.

Ida Bell poured us some coffee, and wasn't doing it in secret like before. Today, she poured it outright for anybody passing by to see. Guess it didn't much matter about secrets anymore. I stirred cream in until my coffee blended in with Ida Bell's skin color so I could look exactly like her. I'd done this a thousand times, but it was real important that I got it right today since I reckoned I'd be living with Ida Bell from now on.

I was itching something terrible to get out to Ida Bell's car. Something told me, though, that the right thing to do was have faith that the kennel cage was there, just as planned. After all, what kind of act of grace wouldn't see itself through? Still, I remembered something. One time my daddy gave a Sunday sermon on putting your whole heart into faith and trust in the good Lord. After Sunday lunch that day, I rode down Daisy Street on my bike. I closed my eyes, and said to that good Lord, "Lord, I have complete faith that I'll be safe riding my bike with my eyes closed. I just know you'll keep me safe." I ran straight into the curb, fell off my bike, and got in trouble with Momma for putting a hole in my pants.

I decided to eat my breakfast a little faster. Maybe, when it was time to go berrying, I could manage to get outside a little bit ahead of Ida Bell. All I needed was a quick peek; I wouldn't even have to open her car door.

"Gracie, now, do tell me what's on your mind. You quiet, and you ain't never quiet!" Ida Bell said.

"All these boxes and running around just got me wanting to get out to the berry patch is all. How is all this gone get done anyway by the time the moving van gets here?"

"Well, now, the movers gone come and do most of it. You know your momma, though. They's some things she gots to do herself. Ain't nobody else gone do it right!" she said, laughing through her nose and shaking her head. "By afternoon time, this place'll be emptied out, all except for the piano, which has to be moved special."

My momma got that piano for her sixteenth birthday, and there was no way in the name of heaven she was gonna allow it on a moving van.

"Gracie, we best get on out to that berry patch before it's so hot the chickens are laying boiled eggs," Ida Bell said. We cleaned up the dishes, and then I said, "Ida Bell, I'll run get our berrying cans and meet you at the oaks," crossing my fingers behind my back that she'd go along. This was my chance to check on my act of grace that was hopefully sitting in her car.

"Thank you, now. I'll be out directly," she said, and I skipped off before something else came up.

❦ 33 ❦

I WENT straight to the garage for our old berrying coffee cans, and then made a point to walk beside Ida Bell's long blue Cadillac on my way out front. Sure as morning light, the dog cage was right where it always was, and my belly got twingy like I was in the waiting room at the doctor's office.

I walked on around front, thinking hard on how everything I did here, I was doing for the last time. The water running through the three-tiered fountain and the wind pushing through the oaks offered a quiet lullaby. Ida Bell came right on out, and I was mighty happy to have her company. "How 'bout we go gets us a keeping-cool drink from the drugstore before we head to the berry patch?" Ida Bell said.

"I'd love to go there one last time, Ida Bell. Let's get the same as usual, you think?"

"Mmm-hmm, I sure do."

We walked along quiet-like. I kicked at street rocks and Ida Bell hummed "Precious Lord" in a soft kind of way. She took my hand in hers, rubbing my hand as we walked. Once we reached the drugstore rocking chairs, little baby whimpers came from a box that read, "Free Puppies." Eight squirming fur balls crawled around inside. Their eyes were open, and every last one of them tried to crawl out of the box to get to us. Water spilled all over the place while the puppies piled one on top of the other.

"Let's take 'em home, Ida Bell! Four for you, and four for me!"

"Honey child, your momma and daddy don't need four more mouths to feed, especially on moving day," she said.

Moving day. Was I forgetting anything important about getting home with Ida Bell? This act of grace business worried me. Like Daddy preached in his sermons, though, "Having faith means believing in a thing that's completely unbelievable. If it is believable, it's not faith you need." All right, Daddy. It was completely unbelievable that I could pull off living with Ida Bell while he and the others moved up the road, so faith was required. *Believe, Grace Callaway, believe, believe, believe, and then believe a little bit more.*

"Ida Bell, look at all the colors in this one little old box!" I'd never laid eyes on such a patchwork quilt of puppies: there was a blond one, a brown one, a black one, a white one, and four with all kinds of color splotches every which way.

"Mmm-hmm, they sure enough pretty little things!" She picked up the blond one on account that one was squishing all the others to get to Ida Bell. "Well, now, ain't you a sight?" The puppy licked Ida Bell square in the face and then nuzzled into her neck.

"Ida Bell, look! This little brown one's chewing sugar-cane like you do!" I wiggled the brown one out from under the others. She was busy with her chewing, but did stop for a second to look up at me. Her head went sideways like she was posing in a puppy magazine. "I gotta have this pup, Ida Bell, and I already know her name: Sugar Bell. *Sugar* for the cane, and *Bell* for you. I ain't leaving her here," I said, my arms folded.

"I sure enough understand, Gracie. I'm getting a little partial to this one here," she said, stroking the blond puppy between the ears. "Kind of reminds me of you, all blond and sweet. I could name her 'Sweetie-G.' Now, wouldn't that be something if you carried home a puppy the color of me named 'Sugar Bell,' and I carried one home looking like you named 'Sweetie-G'?"

"That'd be just perfect, Ida Bell! Aw, look. Sweetie-G sure likes you." That puppy had curled on up and drifted off to sleep in Ida Bell's sweet-smelling neck.

"Well, I 'spect she do. Let's us go on inside and get our drinks. We'll see if these two are still here when we get back. I don't feel terribly sure about your momma and a new puppy on this here particular day, and I don't suppose it'd be right for me to take one if you don't." We lowered Sugar Bell and Sweetie G back down to their busy brothers and sisters, where they both commenced to howling. I looked to see if this tugged at Ida Bell's heartstrings.

"Come on, now, child," she said taking my hand. "If I ain't careful, you'll have me carting this here whole box back down Daisy Street!" I followed Ida Bell on inside the drug-store, but kept my eyes on that puppy box long as I could, and listened for little puppy yelps until the hum of the drugstore took over.

❦ 34 ❦

INSIDE CK's Drugstore, we picked up two bags of peanuts, a couple grape sodas, and a fresh cane stalk for Sugar Bell. A familiar, sing-songy voice rose from behind the counter, "Well, now, Ida Bell and Grace, I have been hoping to see y'all all morning! Let me get a good look at you, little girl. Have you been crying?"

"No, ma'am, Miz Calhoun, I surely haven't." That lady knew good and well I hadn't been crying. She'd do anything to get at somebody else's business. About the last thing I wanted to do on God's green earth was answer her questions, especially because I could see that somebody was out on the porch looking at the puppies.

"Well, tell me, then, are you happy to be moving up to Montgomery? I hear they have right nice property on the Alabama River. Oh, of course you're happy, what with your daddy's distinguished position and all. And what about your momma? Is she interviewing for jobs, and have you found a good, solid church, and reputable schools?"

Ida Bell saved me. "Miz Calhoun," she said, "I'll mention it to Miz Callaway to write to you once she's settled in Montgomery. We gots to be heading on home. Got traveling food warming up in the oven." Ida Bell once told me that a white lie every now and then gives life a little color, long as white-lying don't become a rainbow-like habit.

That lady looking at the puppies walked off talking to an armload of squirmy furballs. I wanted to yell for her to wait, that we just hadn't picked up our puppies yet. The big box was still on the porch, so Ida Bell and me stepped closer. I just couldn't believe my eyes. Two of the cutest little faces in this entire world looked up from that box. It was Sugar Bell and Sweetie-G!

"Well now, your folks might not want four more mouths to feed, but one little old mouth couldn't be too much trouble, I suppose." I hugged and squeezed Ida Bell, letting out a giggle, and then picked up our new puppies. Through sweet-smelling puppy fur, we gave each other our secret handshake.

"All right, Gracie-girl, let's us four head for them berries!" Ida Bell said with a spark. She tucked Sweetie-G under one arm, and jigged with the other, dancing, always dancing. I was feeling so good about my stay-with-Ida-Bell plan and my new puppy that I tucked Sugar Bell under my arm and danced, too. When we came close to the piney woods, the scent of sun-warmed sap settled in my nose, and helped glue my emotions together.

"Ida Bell, can we always come back here, me and you?" She slowed her dancing.

"Oh, I 'spect when you comes down visiting we could slip over here. We gots lots to remember about this here berry patch, now, don't we?" I wanted so bad to tell Ida Bell that I wouldn't need to visit, but I knew better than to make her part of my act-of-grace plan.

"Yes, ma'am. We surely do." I let them piney woods and blackberry brambles fill me up to spilling over. Weaving threads of pine needles through my fingers, I didn't avoid the sappy spots like usual. I let it stick all over my hands where I knew good and well dirt and blackberry juice would settle and like to never come out. The world didn't smell like this in any other spot but this one, I was sure. There was something special about the heat, sap, sweet berries, and the thick greens all around mixed together.

Sugar Bell and Sweetie-G jumped through thickets twice their size. They found a shady spot and piled on each other in spite of the heat for some shut-eye. Ida Bell hummed an introduction, and then we broke into song,

This little light of mine, I'm gonna let it shine
we sang, and then swelled louder and freer into the next stanza,

THIS little light of mine, I'M gonna let it shine
and then our song quieted and slowed,

Let it shine…let it shine…let…it…shine

"Gracie, let's sing it like we sure enough means it. You ready baby girl?"

"Yep." We laid down our coffee cans, and held our arms out to these woods of ours. Eyes closed, our song reached the heavens with its strength. Passersby might've thought we were singing to God; truth was, that song was right straight *from* God.

> *This little light of mine, I'm gonna let it shine.*
> *This little light of mine, I'm gonna let it shine,*
> *Let it shine…let it shine…let…it…shine*

And then our open arms wrapped around each other, pushing that song and these woods and all our memories deep inside for safekeeping. Held inside the strength and softness of her arms, I heard Ida Bell's voice rise again before singing "Precious Lord." This was my listening song, not because Ida Bell said so, but I just couldn't miss out on hearing her voice, deep and stretchy and watery. After humming a little piece of the melody, she sang,

> *Precious Lord, take my hand,*
> *lead me on, let me stand,*
> *I am tired, I am weak, I am worn*

At this part, Ida Bell set her voice loose like a thousand-voice choir, like she was the entire world wrapped up in one person, singing to the heavens.

> *Through the storm, through the night,*

lead me on to the light;
take my hand, Precious Lord,
lead me home

Ida Bell lingered on the mmm in "home," and, without taking a breath, slid right into her part of "Swing Low, Sweet Chariot,"

mmmswing low, sweet chariot
My turn.
Coming for to carry me home
Her again, a little more resolve, a little stretched out.
Swing low, sweet chariot
And then me.
Coming for to carry me home

We went back and forth like this long as we pleased. My mind took me back to Mr. Twilly swinging me from one county to the next. Then to Whet Whetstone, finally carrying himself and his Good Book on up to heaven. And then, to that little angel baby, soft and pink and quiet all wrapped up in the arms of sky, mossy oaks and Alabama sunshine. When Ida Bell joined me on the *coming for to carry me home* part, I knew our song was coming to a close. We let the last words linger on and finish up quiet-like. "Gracie, them Fisk Singers gone be calling us to join they chorus!" Ida Bell said, her eyes dancing.

Our coffee cans were close to spilling, our hands purple as could be. The blackberry juice got wiped all over our berrying clothes, making them even more fit for the task. Sugar Bell and Sweetie-G licked us both as we scooped them up for the walk, and tried their best to swipe our berries. "Well, now, if that don't beat all I ever saw. I never did know a dog would eat blackberries!" Ida Bell said.

"Me, either. These two were meant to be with you and me, clear as morning."

"I reckon you right, Gracie-girl. I reckon you right."

Our arms full-to-bursting with berries, puppies, and memories, we took our final walk home while this was still called ours. My insides, and I mean deep insides, flip-flopped as I walked myself through the coming act of grace, now just a few steps ahead.

🌿 35 🌿

HAVING these two puppies with us on our walk home from berrying turned out to be a stroke of luck. I knew good and well that, without the distraction of them, Ida Bell would've caught on right quick that something was working on my mind. Ida Bell and Sugar Bell were a sight, both heading down Daisy Street with sugarcane hanging out their mouths.

We turned to head through the driveway oaks, and I stopped straight off. Stretched out next to Ida Bell's car was the longest, meanest-looking moving van in this here world. Even the front lights and bumper made a cruel face at me, and gave me an all-over shiver. Seeing that awful thing made me feel for sure and certain about my stay-with-Ida-Bell plan all over again.

"Gracie, what you nodding your head at?" Of course, I didn't mean to be nodding my silly old head as I thought how amazing it was that the act of grace waited for me, so I thought up one of those little white lies that Ida Bell said gives life a little color.

"I'm counting the oaks, Ida Bell. I want to remember each and every one of them."

"Mmm-hmm," she said, but there was a hint of curiosity to her voice. If she'd caught on to my plan, she wasn't telling. It's a strange thing, two folks possibly keeping the same secret from each other. We walked on toward the house, and I snuck another peek inside Ida Bell's long blue Cadillac. I swear, Ida Bell peeked in there, too. The garage was free of boxes, and so was the kitchen. The emptiness hit me hard with the feeling of leaving a place, the *only* place I'd ever called home. Only thing left was the piano in the living room.

Ida Bell and me rinsed our berries with water, then sat down on the floor where the kitchen table used to be. She reached for the little bottle of cream she had brought. After that, she pulled out two little sugar packs. "Now, we can't go eating blackberries without the sweet and the cream!" she said. "Gracie, I gots a mind to enjoy this nice and quiet-like, the way we've done before."

"Me, too, Ida Bell." We took it slow, not wanting our last bowls of Daisy Street blackberries and cream to finish up.

The sound of my momma broke our quiet. "Children, I need all y'all outside and ready to ride. We got the dogs rounded up, and you know they won't stay rounded longer than a minute!" The dogs barely fit in our truck and the one my Daddy's friend drove up for us.

Ida Bell's eyes closed and her head lowered. My forehead beaded up with sweat, and I was scared I was going to throw my blackberries and cream right up. It was getting on time for me to head for that kennel cage. Still, I was a little bit stalled, like a horse wanting to run out the gate, but the gate still good and locked. Ida Bell raised her head and saw me just sitting there, and knew she'd have to be the one to start up the goodbyes.

"Sweet Gracie-girl, they ain't words for certain times, and this here's one of them. Let me squeeze you good, and that'll be our words," Ida Bell said. She hugged me with all of her wide-open heart, and squeezed out the courage I needed to get myself to her car. "I sure do love you, child."

"I love you, too, Ida Bell."

Did my face look as hot as it felt? I goodbyed best as I could, hoping that my eyes looked sad enough that Ida Bell wouldn't catch on to my act-of-grace plan. "I guess I better run before Momma comes looking for me," I said.

Ida Bell didn't say another word, least not with her mouth. Her eyes, deep as the shadowy, cool places in the blackberry woods, held our stories, our secrets, and our hearts, and I don't know how in this world I'd have ever taken mine off them if I thought I was leaving her for good. Sugar Bell and me slipped out, thanking the good Lord everybody else was already out front. We were quick about it, and went straight to Ida Bell's long blue car without a sound. I eased open the back door, unlocked the kennel, then wedged on in. Good thing Sugar Bell and me were small. I was happy to be a ten-year-old wearing clothes made for nine-year-olds. I gave Sugar Bell a fresh cane stalk so she'd keep quiet. My heart thumped so loud, though, that I thought for sure it could give me away. We covered up with blankets and kept still as a steamy pond after a good rain.

36

THANK goodness Ida Bell came quick, or I might've lost my nerve hunched down in the back of her car with my brand new puppy. What but an act of grace could make a person do such a fool thing?

"All right, now, Sweetie-G," Ida Bell said, "You gone ride up here with me this time. Don't be getting all high and mighty, though. I just needs a little company today is all. You gone need to get around in the kennel like all the rest from now on." Ida Bell'd never done that before, least not to my knowledge. This act of grace was in somebody's hands besides my own.

The engine turned, and the windows squeaked as Ida Bell rolled them down to cool the car. We headed down the driveway, and then the turn onto Daisy Street made me steady myself. It felt like we drove straight forever and a day, so I couldn't resist the urge to look and see where we were. I lifted the blanket from my eyes a teeny bit and peeked up out the window. We weren't any farther than Whet Whetstone's! Ida Bell sniffed and it dawned on me that she was letting some of them tears loose that she said a person ought to just let fall and not stop up till the dam breaks. I wanted to shout out to her, *I'm here, Ida Bell, and will be forever,* but I didn't. Sugar Bell and me, we just kept quiet.

Ida Bell drove slow down all of Daisy Street. I knew she was drinking up memories from the dewy air. We passed Harper's.

Were Mother and Daddy looking for me yet?

Close to CK's Drugstore, Ida Bell tuned the radio to 1460 AM. The Blind Boys of Alabama stretched out "Deep River," one of my daddy's favorites. They began in a singing whisper,

Dee-ee-e-eep ri-ver

and then began to swell,

My home is over Jordan

By the end of "Jordan," they were back to quiet. On the next "Dee-ee-e-eep," the Blind Boys broke into a shattering of harmony that sounded more like a choir than it did five little old men singing. The bass singer reached low, I mean real way down low like he was showing how far and deep Earth was from heaven. They sang on,

ri-ver, Lord

The "Lord" note was hung on to from now to eternity, and then they finished the stanza with,

I want to cross over into campground

again breaking into a thousand harmonies at the end. Daddy would've loved how the Blind Boys held onto "Lord," making the Lord the point of it all. He always heard music in a more sacred way than others on account he felt the meanings clearer, deeper. If he was in here with me, he'd sing right along with the Blind Boys, or maybe just close his eyes and feel the Spirit. Momma'd tap her hand on the seat the way she always did at church when the music was especially pretty, and then she'd say, "Listen to that, Peamite…just listen." The Blind Boys still stretched, and my heart could no longer keep time with their easy pace. Before I knew it, I shouted out loud, "Ida Bell, wait a minute!"

Ida Bell hit the brakes. She pulled into the parking lot at CK's Drugstore, got out of the front, unlocked the kennel, and scooped me into her arms like she did when I was a baby. She didn't ask why I was curled up in the kennel, but just acted like I did that all the time. Ida Bell carried me, Sugar Bell, and Sweetie-G to the rocking chairs on the drugstore porch. By the time we got there, my face was coated in snot and tears and sweat. My momma would not have wanted to see me at that moment, sitting here in front of God and everybody else, one soppy, sloppy mess.

"Why do I have to move just because Momma and Daddy say so? Nobody even asked me! Nobody cares what I think but you, Ida Bell, and you're not coming," I said, my voice raising like the red on a thermometer. Then I got an idea I hadn't thought of before, "I know, you come, too! That'd be perfect!"

"Sweet Gracie-girl, now, you know I got children and grandchildren to look after. I gots to stay put," she whispered into my ear while holding me tighter. Ida Bell's rivery eyes looked deeper into me than I believe anyone had ever looked before. I buried my eyes in Sugar Bell's puppy ears, unable to hold in my emotions and Ida Bell's, too. "Honey child, listen real good. And when I get done saying what I gots to say, you listen some more to the quiet that comes after the words. Now, you remember how we took Sugar Bell and Sweetie-G from that box and brought them home?"

"Yes, ma'am," I said, still not able to put my eyes on hers.

"Well, now, they was about to leave all the family they'd ever known, but they wasn't paying that no nevermind. We picked them up, and they nearly wagged their little tails clean off, mm-hmm. I always thought that animals got lots to teach folks about how worrying makes us stop living; now, I know that's true. Honey child, you got all you need right here, and you got all you need up that road," she said and threw her arms around me one last, tight time.

But she didn't let go. "Gracie-girl, we got us some good quiet out on this here porch. Let's listen to it for a while instead of our busy heads and see don't we feel better," Ida Bell said. "Let's listen to sounds at your feet, in your hands, walking close by. Let's listen to sounds way up in the heavens, sounds stuck in the thick air, sounds too far away to hear. Any sound will do, it's the listening that's important, not what you hear."

She held on to me for I-don't-know how long. Listening. Folks came and went from the drugstore, but Ida Bell didn't talk to them like usual. She was with me, and that was it.

I let my mind go still to hear the quiet between all the words and after the words and too far away for words like Ida Bell said. It took me a few tries, but once the jabbering in my head stopped telling me everything wrong about moving away from Ida Bell, I began to hear other sounds. A mockingbird from the top of a tree, Sugar Bell gnawing on cane, the wind winding its way up and around Daisy Street. Calm covered me over, like I rode on that wind up above my worries.

Ida Bell was right: I did have all I needed right here. I didn't quite buy the part about having all I needed up the road, but I did trust Ida Bell. I decided to borrow her faith, since I couldn't quite find my own. Maybe that's some of what Daddy meant in his sermon on faith. Maybe having faith in God sometimes meant trusting in people who love you, especially when your own trust got washed away somehow. Still, I reckon I could have stayed right there in those squeezy arms of Ida Bell's for the rest of my life.

Ida Bell drove me back home, and as we neared the house, she hollered out to Daddy, her fingers crossed behind her back, "Gracie-girl was a sweetie pie to help me with some last-minute things. Y'all have a good ride, now. Be seeing you soon!"

Ida Bell held my hands, her eyes dancing, and needing to say something. "When you get on up that road to your new house, you look for me, cause I'll be there, you gone see. You see a big ol' shady oak, and there I is. Drop some peanuts in your soda pop, and there I is again. You won't believe how much you gone see me! Now, call me right when you get there, you hear?"

"I sure will, Ida Bell. I love you."

"Oh, I love you, too, Gracie. I love you, too." I took in her rosy scent, her warm color, and the glow of her eyes the way a person takes in a long breath of fresh air before heading under water. Ida Bell turned me loose, and I ran toward Daddy. Seemed like I hadn't seen him for a good, long while. We hugged, and I wiped away tears.

"What's this all about?" he asked.

"Just happy to see you is all. This here's Sugar Bell. Ain't she a beauty?"

"She is right pretty! Look at those big feet she's got to grow into. Ruby-Dee'll look after her just fine." Daddy gave Sugar Bell a rub down her back.

"Where's Momma?" I asked.

"She went inside to make sure the piano's all ready for the movers. Wanted to see that the fall board was locked up so the keys don't get damaged on the drive. Want to go see about her?"

"Sure, Daddy. Be right back."

As my feet hit the driveway, one after the other, that night came back to me when I ran home from Whet's after getting my verse from the Good Book. Same as that night, each step I took closer to Momma said a different word, "find . . . grace . . . to . . . help . . . in . . . time . . . of . . . need." *Why didn't my act of grace turn out like it was supposed to?* "Find . . . grace . . . to . . .

help...in...time...of...need." *Why'd I go get a silly old verse in the first place?* "Find...grace...to...help...in...time...of...need. Find..."

"Grace?" Daddy called, but something about the way he said my name right as I was about to think it in my verse made me stop. Grace. Grace! *I* was Grace. Maybe the grace in the verse was meant to have a capital <u>G</u>, and maybe it meant...*me*?

"Gra-aaace?" he called again.

"Yes, sir?"

"Could you get your momma a little water on your way in? She got right hot out here working in this heat."

"Sure will, Daddy." I walked on inside. "It is Well with My Soul" flowed from the piano and filled up that empty house, and I knew right off that it was Momma's hymn-playing. I got a cup from a stack of paper ones left in the kitchen and ran water in it for Momma, then got back to thinking on that verse with the capital G. *Find Grace to help in time of need.* That meant something entirely different from *find grace to help in time of need.* Instead of finding an act of grace to help myself, I *was* the Grace, and was supposed to help somebody else in their time of need. Ida Bell always said that when I was feeling down, the best thing to do was help out somebody else. But who needed help? *My* help?

❦ 37 ❦

I SAT down on the stairs to listen in on Momma's playing. She'd surely stop the very minute she knew I was there. High little quiet notes flowed from her fingers and tickled my heart. She was still playing her own made-up version of an introduction, a bit of the refrain before the first stanza, and it was soft and pretty, all played on the top treble keys of her childhood piano. She held on to the last note of the introduction so long that I wondered if this was where the song would stop this time; instead, she transitioned on into the first stanza, still timid little high strikes with flowy treble accompaniment,

When peace, like a river, attendeth my way

Then she dropped an octave lower and let the crescendo mound up like a distant storm rolling in,

When sorrows like sea billows roll

Momma played the first *When sorrows like* in its usual tempo, but the *sea billows roll* part was pulled out with a tension like a real turbulent sea. Momma added deep bass notes that gave the feeling of thunder and fear. And then in the notes between these words and what would come next, Momma's hands went in opposite directions, filling up the entire piano and swelling the whole wide world with tune and feeling. Just when I thought the song was as big as big could get, Momma played even louder, even fuller,

Whatever my lot, Thou has taught me to say

Toward the end of this phrase, Momma gave the notes the littlest perfect bit of quiet.

Then, nothing. All this, and Momma just stopped before the glorious part. Why did Momma's songs not ever get finished? Instead of her playing the part that comforts the listener, there were quiet sniffs like a shy little girl being teased. I peeked around the corner to see tears in streams down her face, and I saw my momma, I mean truly saw her, for the first time in my life. There she was with all her memories of her daddy, all her stress from the welfare department, and from her own fiery momma. Right off, it hit me. This was my chance, and it may be my only chance. *Momma* was the one who needed me. I was the Grace who was supposed to help *her* in time of need.

Without one speck of hesitation, I went right straight to her. I sat beside her on the bench, and began finishing the song that always hung incomplete. That must be what she needed, for me to help her finish up her song when she couldn't do it herself. That sounded like grace to me.

Then Momma surprised me. She took the bass while I kept the treble. Together, we got through the refrain, the resolution, the comfort, and started to finish that song Momma'd been trying to complete all alone for as long as I could remember. Together was a whole different story from alone. The sound of us filled the room and quieted our bended, blended hearts.

Sitting there beside Momma, she became more than *my momma*. In the first place, she wasn't *mine*. A person don't own another person. And in the second place, I realized that she was a lot of things besides my momma. I saw the little girl she used to be, sitting in front of her daddy's country store getting treated like a princess. I saw her as a daughter at the whims of her own momma's clenched hands. I saw the sister in her who raised her own little brother. I saw her as friend to people with dirt under their nails, and to some who sparkled when they walked on account of all their drippy diamonds. I saw her as a friend to folks with no sparkle or spark at all. In those moments, the air all filled with song, I picked up Momma's pain, held it up to the light, and then looked up under it. There was the child momma once was. And there was the child that was me. Right under there, folded up under my Momma's wings.

Things were different between me and Momma in that moment, and I knew they would be forever. It wasn't as easy as before to find the line drawn between me and her. Did

Momma actually end somewhere, and then I began? If there was a line at all between us, it was a blurry one. There we were, playing the same song, four hands on the piano, two hearts creating the swells of feeling, one spirit between us both.

After the last *It is well with my soul*, Momma and me sat still, neither of us wanting to end being able to really feel each other after so long acting like each of us was all alone. Momma kept on crying, her tears of sorrow all mixed up with new tears of love. I cried, too, and my momma and me sat at her old piano together for a while. Really and truly together.

BENEDICTION

PEOPLE are always saying love is this or love is that. I'm pretty sure love means different things in different times for different people. In my momma's case, love meant she was totally accepted and that she belonged, never being judged in the past, not judging her in the present, and not trying to make her a certain way. For Daddy, love was our total acceptance of Momma. And in Ida Bell's case, love required nothing at all. Not a single, blessed thing, maybe because she *was* love itself, like water not getting thirsty for water.

We drove away from Daisy Street that afternoon for the last time. During the 82-mile trip, Ida Bell was all over the place, just like she said she'd be. She was in the daisies that glowed in the dark as the sun went down, in the lingering sweet after my sugarcane was all gone, and in the wild blackberry thickets by the roadside. I realized that Ida Bell's soul, the spirit of her, couldn't all be kept in her one body. Her spirit was bigger than that.

I got to thinking, too, on that drive, that there was more to my momma than what I could see with my eyes. She floated through the air with the music from her hymn-playing. She was in her tears that fell on her daddy's grave, and in the brilliant blue of the heavy hydrangea, so full of bloom they bowed. I thought of Whet Whetstone when we passed by a country church, and of that beautiful angel baby in the pink evening glow on the clouds up high. All these reminders of Ida Bell, Momma, Whet Whestone, and the angel baby weren't just reminders. They were them. Actually and really and truly *them*.

As we drove up the Deep South, I looked into the sky, way beyond the deepest deeps where voices don't use words. The night sky was painted in the poetry of Ida Bell's eyes. I knew I'd wonder where Ida Bell was, what she was doing, from time to time for as long as I lived. I also knew that she was everywhere I was, always, right in the middle of my very own heart.

CPSIA information can be obtained at www.ICGtesting.com
Printed in the USA
LVOW11*1255201015

458984LV00004B/4/P

LONGWOOD PUBLIC LIBRARY
800 Middle Country Road
Middle Island, NY 11953
(631) 924-6400
mylpl.net

LIBRARY HOURS

Monday-Friday	9:30 a.m. - 9:00 p.m.
Saturday	9:30 a.m. - 5:00 p.m.
Sunday (Sept-June)	1:00 p.m. - 5:00 p.m.